WHISPERS IN THE DARK

GAYLE EDEN

WHISPERS IN THE DARK
Published by Linden Bay Romance, 2006
Linden Bay Romance, LLC, U.S.
ISBN # 1-905393-40-7

Edited by *M. Morpeth*
Cover art by *Beverly Maxwell*

Chapter 1

The Earl of Wythe stood in the center of his chamber, his valet having departed only moments earlier after assisting him into his formal clothing. With only one lamp burning from the adjoining sitting room, moonlight spilled through the window, striking his swarthy face and midnight eyes, glinting on the wavy black hair that settled at his shoulders.

Lord Roger was that enticing contrast between rake and gentlemen, the expert cut of his clothing, the stark white cravat, the musculature and height, the dark skin, reflecting something forbidden and wicked. It echoed in the curve of his full lips, the flair of his nostrils, the winged arch to his brows and a scar that ran from below his right eye to the under-curve of his jaw.

Smoke curled from the cheroot he was enjoying, his expression reflecting deep thought, and his firm jaw set in lines that hinted they weren't pleasant ones. He had so many women, so easily and the fact that one had cost him a moment's discomfort was a rare and unique experience indeed. He was determined to rid himself of this irritation.

Joan… Joan Lecrox. He tasted the name in his mind, as he had tasted her lips… *just before she'd slapped him.*

Roger laughed suddenly, a short grunt of it, before he shook his head and crushed out his cheroot. He gathered his gloves and cape, found his cane, and walked out of the room, into the upper hall, before descending the spiral staircase.

"Have a pleasant evening, my lord." His butler Kingsly bowed while handing him his hat. Roger stepped out with a murmur of thanks. His coach was waiting. He eased himself inside, settling back against the plush leather and rested his hands atop his cane. The driver pulled out and they began their journey.

1

Tonight was not a usual theater night for him. In fact, he was going to miss several appointments attending the play, not the least of which was a night with an actress who wanted to share his bed. Actually, since meeting the maddeningly *hard to seduce* Joan Lecrox.

Near the theater the expected crush of carriages and milling people clogged the entrance. His driver stopped at a good space, and Roger exited, flinging his cape over his shoulder while he stood back from the crowd to eye the patrons at length.

The usual ton were always easy to spot in their glitter and furs. He had been on the scene many years and was well aware, and totally unfazed, by the fact that the high sticklers bit their tongue around him, because of his wealth and title. In truth, they had their pets amid the rakes and rogues. At thirty-four he had been in their circle long enough to let them know he neither cared nor sought their approval. He accepted invitations when the mood struck him, and indulged his own interest when it did not, as they were apt to do. He was a man who'd spent enough time abroad in mixed cultures to have explored and experimented with whatever took his interest…and very little of those interests were perused amid the ton.

"Wythe!"

Roger turned his gaze to the right and nodded, smiling slightly at the urbane and wholly rumpled Viscount Berrenger.

"Simon," he drawled deeply. "What brings you out before the stroke of midnight?"

The lanky viscount pushed away from the outer wall and strolled over. His cravat undone, and his over-long sable hair wind blown. He flashed Roger a cynical smile. "A request from my cousin."

"Cousin?"

Simon stared at him. "Joan Lecrox."

2

Roger's brow rose. He had known the Viscount for years, they had slummed, and gambled, together but Simon never spoke of family besides his elderly father.

"Yes." Simon seemed to read his mind and appeared amused. "It seems she requires the added protection of a male relative—"

"Rather like the fox guarding the fox, wouldn't you say?" Roger cut him off.

"It's none of my business whom you seduce or vise versa," Simon muttered flatly. "But Joan is off limits." Simon eyed Roger's hard set jaw and added with a mild smile, "Should you, however, decide to court her...that would, of course, alter things greatly."

Roger's dark eyes narrowed. "Are you jesting perchance? I could quite easily list a number of..."

"Don't bother. Yes, I've seduced my share of the fair sex. I'm no hypocrite. 'Tis merely that...Joan is off limits."

"You said that before," Roger told him, his voice clipped. "Would you care to expound on it while we make our way to *your* box?"

Simon laughed. "Don't make this difficult. I've boxed and fenced with you, ole boy. I would prefer you make this unpleasant chaperone business easier for me. I do so detest these sorts of noble roles and family obligations."

They'd begun to walk forward, and Roger said, "You were going to tell me why she's off limits?"

"Was I?" Simon yawned.

Roger stopped and several people had to walk around them. He waited with a black scowl for Simon to realize he was serious.

"Because she's no deb, and she's not of the fast set. She's got a mind of her own and she's settled in it, that you are merely out to seduce her...smart gel that she is. Though she's lived in the country with her books and herbs and what not, she knows me well enough to call me a rake, and, while my exploits might amuse and irritate

3

her, she said, and I quote, *You keep the rest of your bloody crowd away from me.* Simon smiled and shrugged. "There you go, ole boy. A direct command."

Roger grunted. They entered the foyer with its din of voices and scent of cigars. People were gathered in little groups talking, chatting, and rubbing elbows. He returned, "Lead the way."

"Give over, Rog," Simon groaned. "I've said I hate this bloody role. Inviting you to my box is really going to have Joan at my throat."

"You'll live."

"She slapped you."

Roger glanced at him. "Umm, yes."

Simon grunted. "Well, she might not slap you tonight, but I'll sure get a tongue lashing should you insist on this."

"I insist."

"Bloody hell." Simon reached over, took someone's drink and downed it. He coughed and wheezed to Roger. "Why are these female cousins always orphaned?"

Roger smiled at his question. "She must be twenty-two at least. I should think that puts her in the status of adulthood."

"She's twenty four."

"Really."

"Yes." They went through the draped exit and entered his box. His cousin Joan was already seated with her companion Miss Avery.

~

She couldn't believe it! Absolutely, she was going to murder Simon.

Joan Lecrox turned from having glanced at the entry, fixing her eyes on the stage whilst she tried to control her temper. *Damn, Simon.* She had thought for sure that he would honor her request and not bring the bloody man within inches of her. And, there he was. She was aware he'd taken the seat behind her.

4

Simon touched her shoulder to get her attention. Joan smacked his hand with her fan, hard, and did not turn around. She'd like to beat him about the head with it. Honestly. She was going to kill him. She considered getting up and just walking out, but the orchestra had signaled and the crowd from the foyer was entering boxes and getting settled. The lights were going down...

Joan unfurled her fan and turned her head slightly to eye Simon, who was seated just behind her companion. He must have caught the movement for he leaned up and tried again.

"I didn't invite him, puss. He was rather insistent, and believe me, I know the man. He would have caused a scene and cared little about it."

"I'm not speaking to you," she hissed back. "I'm never speaking to you again."

Simon chuckled. "Have a heart. You should have picked a good cousin for this task...I've known Rog for years."

"I don't have a good cousin, you wretch...I have only one, you...no, I take that back. I disown you. Feel free to leave at any time."

Simon sighed loudly. She heard him say to Lord Wythe. "You see, ole man. Now you have gotten me in the suds. I am completely disowned."

Lord Roger's deep, somewhat raspy voice intoned, "Your cousin is being rather extreme over a mere kiss."

Joan turned the other way to regard the dark lord. "How dare you mention that!"

That sensual mouth twisted in a smile, and even with the low lighting she could see his dark eyes shimmering. "I dare many things, Joan..."

"I can see that," she bit out. "And since you had your face slapped for doing so with me, I should think you'd get the message."

"What would that be?"

"I'm no fool, Lord Wythe. I'm here for one season as a courtesy to my uncle. I may not be London bred, but I've read and heard enough about you to know exactly what your game is. Play it somewhere else."

Roger stared at that face. It wasn't ravishing, nor exactly beautiful with her green eyes glittering with anger and that almost too-wide mouth set in hard lines. She had a proud nose, angled chin and unfashionable light freckles on her cheeks that she did not bother to hide with powder. Her hair was slightly curly, likely a mere shoulder's length, and since she did no more than hold it back with combs, the curls were escaping at her temples and by her ears. He had seen more ravishing females. But it wasn't looks, not even the challenge, it was…an odd sort of chemistry that flared from the first time he'd encountered her taking air on the balcony at the Lamont's ball…and kissed her.

From where he sat a foot behind her, he could smell that scent, the mixture of woman and heat and some dark night flower that he couldn't name. He'd had sex with many forgettable females, and not one of them had drawn him like Joan Lecrox.

Roger was no green lad. He did not play games, as she put it. He followed impulse, he satisfied hungers. He knew what rumors she'd heard, though his privateering days were behind him and they were the least of the dark whisperings linked to his name. She was doubtless referring to the rumors that his parents had disowned him years before they had died, and the woman he'd been betrothed to from a tender age had fled to Paris to escape a so-called nightmare union with him when he'd retired from the sea.

He said though, neither cynically nor harshly, but in a whisper, "I am well beyond games, Joan."

He saw her eyes widen slightly, her cheeks flush before she gathered her composure and returned, "I am sure you have plenty of women, my lord, who more than welcome your attention. Pray, do not waste your time with me. I have no intention of giving you a moment of it."

Mentally he smiled at her pluck, for no woman to his knowledge would dare spar with him. "Then I shall have to take it."

Her lips parted; she blinked.

He laughed softly. "No. To the contrary of the rumors you may have heard, I never developed a taste for...force. Seduction is much more satisfying."

"You're beyond belief," she hissed. "Now, please. We are in a public place. If you persist in this folly, I shall leave."

He was outright chuckling now.

Joan wanted to slap him again. He was trying to shock her. She knew that. The man was provoking her, and he was totally without manners. The drama began on stage and she turned, after shooting Simon a harsh look. She settled her eyes on the actors, and felt Lord Wythe's remain on her for far too long a time. There was a hot sensation, over the back of her neck and her shoulders. If not for the fact she knew he'd mock it, she would have lifted her shawl from her elbows and covered herself. She heartily wished she'd worn a less fashionable gown, the bodice of the jade velvet dress was low, and off the shoulder. There were more beautiful woman, more exposed ones too, to look at, *why didn't he bloody seduce them instead?*

For Joan, it was too long a play, and too long between acts. Twice she got up to leave, and twice she found Lord Roger standing in her way. She hated the fact that sitting down reeked of admitting defeat, it gave the impression she would bow to his insistent plan of being near her. But she sat there chewing her lip by the last act, having no alternate route of escape.

When the curtain closed, she nudged her companion awake, resisting the urge to roll her eyes at the woman's drooling snores. Miss Avery was her uncle's choice, because frankly, in the country, no one gave a fig if Miss Lecrox went about with only a maid, or even by herself. In Bristol, she had lived since the age of nineteen, completely on her own.

Simon had stood too. He muttered to her, "I don't suppose I'm escorting you home?"

"No." She eyed his rumpled clothing. "Don't bother to take my request seriously hereafter, Cousin. You are bloody rotten at it."

"I'm still a cousin at least." He winked.

She sniffed. "Do go on, and take your friend with you."

Simon bowed and headed for the exit. Joan saw, to her dismay, that her companion had sleepily followed. The stupid woman left her standing there with Lord Roger.

He was tall. She had noticed that at the ball, noted it on the balcony when he'd nearly lifted her off the floor. Standing a bit back from him, she still had to look up, and when the lights came up, there was that shadow around him, those piercing blackish eyes and that dark skin.

Joan pulled her wrap up over her shoulders and detected several scents coming from him, *all too dark and masculine to want to name at the moment.*

"Do you intend to let me pass?"

He was gazing over her face—her body too. "Allow me to escort you home."

"Are you bloody joking?" She spurted laughter.

His lips curved. "Joan, you may as well give an inch or two."

"I have my own coach."

"Mmm. I'll send him ahead, with your companion."

"I'm not being alone in any coach with you."

That seemed to amuse him. "I intend to at least have a conversation with you, so you may as well give in."

"We have nothing to say to each other." She made to step around him.

8

His tawny hand came out, catching her upper arm. She stumbled a bit as he drew her close to him, her shoulder touching his chest. He leaned down, whispering in that raspy husk, "I want you, Joan."

My God...those words somehow turned to fingers of fire that trailed from her ears, down her spine. They settled in her blood, leaving it pounding with the beat of her heart.

"I don't want you," she said gruffly, staring away from him.

His thumb brushed her skin. He murmured, "Are you a virgin?"

She jerked her eyes to his face. "Do you want your face slapped again?"

"Ah, no." He laughed, flashing her a rare white smile. "I think you enjoyed it too much."

"I'd enjoy it immensely now too."

That smile lingered though he led her toward the exit, keeping a hold on her all the way through the lobby. When they were out in the crush, he leaned down and told her softly, "I'll give you this round, sweet."

To her embarrassment he removed his hand from her arm, but brushed it down her spine before he told her, "Go now, Joan."

Left standing stupidly alone, she watched his figure stride down toward a cluster of crested coaches.

"Miss?"

Joan snapped out of her haze, glancing at her driver on his perch. She ducked into the coach after the theater footman opened the door. Inside, she settled her skirts, noting with some disgust that Miss Avery was fast asleep. The coach turned. Joan absently looked out the window, somehow not at all surprised when fate had them stopping to allow for traffic whilst alongside Lord Wythe's vehicle.

He had his arm along the window edge and was already looking right at her. Those pitch eyes seeming to burn with hidden fires.

Joan licked her lips and wished she had not, for a slight smile suddenly played about his mouth and his lashes dipped. When Henri had the coach moving, she let out a long breath.

Chapter 2

She wasn't a coward. That's what Joan told herself for the next week, whilst she holed up like a rabbit. The house she'd rented was just on the edge of a fashionable address, a concession her uncle, Simon's father, had made to get her to come to London.

Joan spent much of that week sitting in the window seat, reflecting, and doing it out of sheer boredom. She actually was an active person. In spite of the fact her mother had been Lady Anna Lecrox, she and Joan's father had lived a very normal, very open-to-change life, where normalcy meant the simple things like attending the parish church, sailing, walking, gadding about the countryside, and of course, exploring everything from art to books and sciences.

It wasn't an unusual home life by any means; lots of country folk lived a world apart from the ton. People actually were quite free of most of the strictures. Parties and picnics, weeklong celebrations were lively, interesting. Absolutely nothing like Joan dreaded, and found, the London scene to be. Her mother had told her, described it, and she'd wanted Joan to experience it. But when Joan kept putting it off, and did so until her parent's death, her uncle had stepped in and picked up the prodding. Never mind that she was no deb, an old maid by ton standards, good ole Uncle Willy insisted she must have a taste of the ton before she settled into permanent oldmaidship.

In her reflecting, Joan wryly thought of Lord Wythe's question about her virtue. It was rather startling to be asked so bluntly. She didn't know that people could tell such things, well, unless a person was morally loose in their behavior or some such.

Joan wasn't. She considered herself mature however, and a secure and levelheaded woman. *Oh all right*, she'd let the truth surface about mid week whilst she was looking out that window and watching the world move on.

There was a time at the age of seventeen when she'd fancied herself in love. Her mother despaired of her; her poor papa was at his wit's end, for the most biddable and sensible daughter suddenly turned into a stranger. She snorted in disgust thinking of it.

The man was older—she hadn't cared. He was a cad—she hadn't cared. He'd been after her virtue and her fortune—she hadn't cared. Nothing mattered, and the entire year seemed like a blur of space, where now, thinking on it, she'd totally lost her head. Suffice it to say, her father had put an end to it, and rightly so. He'd beat him to a bloody pulp, paid the fellow a hefty sum, and sent him off on a long trip abroad. Her mother's attitude helped Joan get over the truth when it smacked her between the eyes. *She was no longer a virgin*, was most certainly feeling like a fool, and as Anna said, there was no use dwelling on what could not be undone. She must simply learn from it and move on.

Ha! *Oh yes, she had learned*, perhaps become a cynic, or close to it. She'd educated herself about men, their ways, and God knew, she did not trust her body as a guide. She understood attraction, had felt it many, many times, but the kind of sex she'd allowed with Robert Gilmore, the bloody wretch, was not worth the anticipation. And, it was only two years later that her mother had finally had a frank and open talk about it. At nineteen, the year they had died, she'd told her mother what an awful, awkward, and wholly unsatisfying intimacy she'd had with Robert. From her mother's answers, she knew he'd been selfish, uncaring about anything but his own pleasure, and that he'd used her.

That knowledge did not help a great deal. It only explained the irritation she'd begun to feel, the coldness, just before her father had stepped in and ended the thing. Somewhere along the line she'd already been snapping out of that girlish fantasy, getting a dose of the real world, where sex did not always equal intimacy or pleasure.

She'd realized that having it with every man she was attracted to, would ultimately lead to that empty and used feeling again. She understood, though, why men could have such associations; after all, they did not need the closeness, the true intimacy that females desired. They didn't need love in the mix.

Was she attracted to Lord Roger? She asked herself this on Friday. *Yes*, she also answered herself. The problem was, it was not a logical attraction. It made not a whit of sense to her. She'd heard about him for years, who had not? Dark sorts of tales, mysterious murmurings, that fit his scarred face and black eyes. She did not doubt that tales of his sexual prowess were true, any more than she doubted he'd been a privateer. About his fiancée running off? Who knew. Men of his ilk were not so abundant, not in looks, manner or reputation, that she had any experience whatsoever dealing with them.

Drat! This was her word on Saturday as the walls were closing in and she had her mare saddled for a ride in the park. She would never make it through the season like this. *Why was the man attracted to her at all?* She was too old, not exactly attractive, her body was, well it was fine with her, but it was nothing extraordinary. *Pahh...* She went below dressed in her green habit with black jabot and jaunty hat. She was not so dramatic as the debs and other females she'd heard whispering about him. She did not fear him in some sinister way. He was just a man.

Somehow though, riding along Rotten Row amid the ton an hour later, she admitted that though fear was not it, there was something about him that threw her off balance, which was why she pretended to be much braver and daring, at least vocally, than was her norm. She had to keep him at arm's length.

"Good afternoon, Joan."

Bloody hell! Joan both saw and felt the massive black stud nudging against her mare. That deep voice was not cheerful, but rather smooth and warm.

"My lord." She nodded without looking at him, sure that everyone would note that their mounts were nearly side to side. She grit her teeth as the beast used his stronger mount to nudge her mare off the path, and toward the tree line.

Flexing her gloved hands on the reins she looked at him when it was impossible to ignore him. He'd led her completely off the path.

"Have you had a pleasant week of rest?"

"Yes." She let her gaze scan his dark face, noting that amused curve to his lips.

"Joan." His dark eyes caught and held hers. "You really should not fear me. There's no reason to go to ground."

"I don't fear you. I simply do not wish to see, speak, or be around you."

He let his gaze run slowly down her and then back up, saying softly, "My looks do not bother you?"

"There's nothing wrong with your looks, as you well know," she snapped.

"Do I? Have you per chance, not heard of the names the youn-"

"Yes," she cut him off just as dryly. "I know what the silly debs and gossips call you. But then, we're speaking of a society that relishes drama and dictates what hair, eye color, or gown is all the rage." Joan allowed her own gaze to wander over his all-black clad form, not allowing herself to linger on the wide shoulders or the cut of muscle visible from the snug fit of his riding breeches. "You're a rake, Lord Roger. Just as Simon is. And you've both been very diligent to earn such a label. Why you imagine that *I* would welcome your attentions, I do not know."

He was full out smiling, and it irritated her.

"You're very blunt speaking, Joan. Do you always tell the truth?"

"I try."

14

"Hmm." He nodded, still grinning. "It is quite refreshing."

"To be rejected?" she smiled fake. "I'm sure it is, for you."

He laughed. "You are going to draw this out, aren't you?"

"No. You're going to find another distraction." She looked around to avoid staring at his smile. "I could give you a list of names, if you like, of more willing debs, or even some women my age, beauties, with more money, more interest, and less common sense."

"Look at me."

She obeyed because of the very softness, the hush of his command. She wished she had not. His face was quite still, but his eyes were like banked fires.

In a smooth murmur he told her, "I am not blind. I have seen them all, had a few dozen, but I want you."

"Well, that is too bad. You can't have me." She couldn't manage more than a whisper.

"Ah, Joan..." He let his gaze move over her face. "I would have you in ways that would make that little kiss I stole, seem like a mere touch." He held her gaze. "Your eyes are a deeper green than the leaves...they shimmer. Do you know that? "

She didn't. But she husked, "Why?"

He seemed to know what she was asking. He said softly, "You are far from unattractive, Joan. I like your scent, your voice, the way you move, the way you look when you are angry...why not?"

"Because for all I am on the shelf, according to the ton, I am not the kind of woman to indulge in an affair."

"So, you are a virgin?"

"No." She looked him in the eye. "And neither am I a whore or worse. I was young once, a foolish little girl who made a mistake. But I will not make it again, anymore than I will consider myself forever stained by that youthful indiscretion. It is perhaps fortunate that I do not have to

15

please the ton, nor am I here to find a husband. My parents left everything they had to me, and where I live my life, who or what I am, is not something I worry about, because beyond this city, people live in reality."

Roger stared at her for several moments before saying, "I applaud your maturity. My question was not based on judgement, few men of my reputation can cast stones, nor do I care one way or the other. I thought to judge, however, if your refusal was based on that."

She shook her head. "My lord, I am being totally honest with you. I will not entangle myself in an affair with a man such as yourself. I think, that you know why."

His jaw tightened.

"It is a game to you, Roger." She deliberately dropped his title. "It is a challenge. And, attraction or not, you can walk away unscathed when you tire of it, or me." She turned her mare and looked over her shoulder at his dark face. "Does anyone know you? Do they really?"

He did not answer but his lashes flickered as if to hide some emotion.

Joan smiled slightly. "Temptation is not exclusive to men. Desire and attraction, we all feel it. You cheat yourself, my lord, rumors aside, and you have lived a very long time avoiding intimacy. No doubt, you are skilled and have vast experience. But I did learn the hard way, that without intimacy, I can easily resist attraction or temptation."

"It is rather difficult to get to know someone you deliberately avoid."

She had to laugh, but said, "You made your goal too obvious. You were, *are,* rather blunt."

"A trait we share."

She sighed and turned back around, looking toward the path. "You do not want to get to know me, Roger. You want to seduce me."

"True...about the seduction. However, I see that it hasn't worked thus far." He came alongside her and stopped. "Why are you not husband-hunting?"

She glanced at him. "Is that a way of asking me if I equate intimacy with marriage?" She added, "My parents had a good one, I hope whomever I wed that we'll have that. For certain I will not marry a man without it. But I am aware, very much so, that men desire their wives pure, ignorant and submissive, and I am aware, that a man can gain my inheritance. My mother was very candid with me and my eyes are open to the unions I've observed. I have no need of a husband, to answer your question. But I *do not* desire to have an affair."

He appeared to consider that. "Your first lover was not a good one."

She stared at him, feeling exasperated. "No, likely not. A selfish one who used me, whom my father paid off... after he bloodied his nose and a few other things. But that's not relevant. I'm well over it. It's simply that I'd be a fool to forget what that mistake showed me about myself."

He rode alongside her until they were on the path again. For some reason she found herself asking, "Will you not have to wed, for an heir?"

"I have a distant cousin somewhere who would likely fit the title, and the ton, far better than I have."

"Is it true, that your parents disowned you?"

He cocked a brow at her. "Yes." Then laughed shortly. "You are the first person to ask me that."

"Really?"

"Really." He nodded and conversation paused while riders passed by them. When they were side by side again, he said, "They died before the war was over and, to m'father being a privateer was equal to piracy. I was not free to talk about my missions and outside the war, those who knew in government, could not correct rumor and accusation..."

"That must have been difficult," she mused aloud. "And your intended? Is that why she fled w—"

"No. Maria was not overjoyed to be linked to me, because of the rumors, and my scars repulsed her. But she fled with a man who would give her what I refused to."

"What is that?"

"She wanted to honor the betrothal, to wed, without sharing my bed."

"Oh."

He grunted. "I did not require she give me an heir, nor did I need her fortune. But would not be manipulated into a marriage that she desired solely for the title, and my wealth."

"I do not blame you."

"Don't you?"

She glanced at him. "Don't mock. I'm perfectly serious. You would gain absolutely nothing, and to live with someone who held you in aversion…" she shrugged. "It wouldn't be the reason you seem to have an abundance of women since then, would it?"

He laughed. "No. I quite enjoy sex."

Her cheeks flushed. "Mmm."

"A blush? Joan, I thought you far too mature for that."

She laughed. "I may well be, but men, most of them, do not speak the way you do."

"I prefer to be frank."

"I noticed."

They had come to the gates and beyond it her groom waited with the carriage.

Joan gave him a final glance. He apparently was not departing as yet.

"Do we understand each other now?"

He half smiled.

"Rake." She shook her head. "Do find someone more cooperative, Roger. I promised Uncle I would do the season, and I detest taking the coward's way and running home to avoid you."

"Then don't avoid me, Joan."

Rolling her eyes, she wheeled and went through the gate, choosing to ignore his deep laughter behind her.

Chapter 3

"Gave up, did you?" Simon eyed Roger lazily, having walked into the dockside tavern and spied him at a corner table.

"I see you have no black eyes." Roger moved his arm as the serving wench sloshed beer on the table, attempting to set down the tray, and yell crudely back at a drunken sailor who'd been trying to feel her up for the past hour.

"My eyes are fine, but my ears are blistered." Simon removed his cape and sat down, pulling off the dangling neck cloth and tucking it into his pocket. He helped himself to Roger's beer, then took a long pull. "You really should simply mark her down as a loss, Rog. Even I draw the line somewhere, and I'll admit, it's damned uncomfortable, knowing what I do of you, to simply give you leave to seduce my cousin."

"Your cousin, is well able to speak for herself."

Simon snorted. "Don't I know it. I stooped to going round with flowers and sweets. Called upon her this morning. She called me everything but a cousin."

Roger smiled at that.

"Don't look so smug. She called you a few things too."

"I'm certain she did."

"There's bets at Whites about it." Simon sat back and lit a cheroot. "Not that you're subtle or hide your...um, exploits, but riding in the park with her... You've given rise to talk."

"That's hardly new to me." Roger lit his own cheroot, his eyes scanning the crude interior and shabby patrons.

There were a few gents playing cards or making sport with some of the wenches. He was a bit choosier than that. He had seen too many sailors, lords too, with the pox. No man with a brain would indulge his lusts without ample knowledge of how to prevent both it and unwanted bastards. England may be a powerful country, but there were other places in the world, far more advanced in such things than his own culture.

Simon, also a sophisticated man of the world, was apparently thinking along the same lines when he muttered, "Young Pendleton is about to get more than he's paying for."

"Yes." Roger turned away from the scene and sipped his beer. The wench was already astride the young viscount, providing entertainment for a group of patrons who were yelling and laughing and calling out crudely. Jaded he was, but performing for a bunch of drunken sailors escaped him.

Simon too turned away and simply raised a brow toward Roger, both of them having witnessed that and baser acts in the taverns and gin houses and alleyways. Since Simon had served in the Navy, he was as versed as Roger on the dark side, the strange tastes men and women sometimes had concerning lust. They didn't discuss it, because it was none of their affair.

When the din grew louder Simon muttered, "Are you interested in leaving?"

"Yes." Roger tossed some coins out on the table and they left. He knew that things of that nature could lead to more acts he had no wish to see.

Their cape collars up, they sent Roger's coach home and instead climbed into Simon's carriage, telling the man to drive around. They sat facing each other while the sounds of night mingled with the clop of hooves and churn of carriage wheels.

"You did not answer my question."

Roger glanced at Simon. "No."

"No you didn't answer—or no you've not given up?"

"It's none of your business."

Simon slumped in the seat, putting his booted feet in the other. "It isn't. But I'm damned curious. You've not attended a single thing Joan has this week."

Roger eyed him, amused. "Your own raking should leave little time for keeping track of me, Simon."

"My sins are as numerous this week as last." Simon yawned. "But 'tis a damned fine bit of distraction to an otherwise boring season."

"I thought you were supposed to be playing protector?"

"You said yourself, she can speak her own mind. I'm not assisting you however. I happen to like m'cousin, even if she is female. What few times we were in company over the years, I have found her surpassingly interesting, and she reminded me this morning, of the day I taught her to shoot."

"You did?"

"Yes. And she reminded me in the process of telling me that she ought to prove to me how exemplary an instructor I was, for leaving you with her at the theater."

Roger laughed.

Simon cocked his brow. "That amuses you, does it?"

"Yes. She does."

"Ah…" Simon crossed his arms and tilted his head slightly, studying Roger in the moonlight. "That is telling."

Roger glanced out and then back. "Don't strain yourself trying to make it something it isn't. I have no hostility toward women, and other than the normal irritation with silly debs or old gossips, or a bitchy mistress, I don't have, as the gossips claim, some lingering bitterness toward the sex because of Maria."

"Then why don't you wed and beget heirs."

"Because I do not have to." Roger lit another cheroot and settled back. "And one must try and be discreet when one marries, or should, I expect…"

Simon stared at the toes of his boots. "Yes, there is that."

The driver was nearing St. James when Roger asked, "How is it that she is so independent?"

22

"Father says she is just like her mother was. Anna was brought up the same as any deb, but had too much spirit and too much intellect to be content in that circle. Soon as she found the man she loved, she thumbed her nose at the whole crowd and settled in one of the country estates." He brushed his long hair back when it blew in his eye and went on, "Uncle was a great gun too. He was a sportsman, and I seem to recall he laughed a lot, at least, my aunt seemed to amuse him. They were oddly close, comfortable you might say, and very unlike the ton. My stays with them were few, but relaxed. I do recall Joan doing as much with her father as with my aunt. I don't think Uncle raised her to be anything but herself."

"Unusual."

"Yes. My father said, that he pried Cousin out of the country, because Joan was too interesting a woman for some squire or merchant."

"She told me she wasn't husband-hunting."

"I know that. But my father is still old fashioned in many ways."

"You must give him gray hair?"

"Every one of them, or so he likes to tell people." Simon smiled.

The carriage stopped before Roger's house. As he was getting out Simon offered, "Have you considered, Rog, that this attraction is more than…well, an attraction?"

"No." Roger closed the door and shot him a look. "Go see your mistress, Simon, you are beginning to sound much too principled."

Later in his chamber, Roger sat by the window wearing only his trousers and sipping a bracing whiskey. He was not exactly focusing on the moonlit view, but rather looking inward and replaying that day in the park. He told himself that he was merely changing his tactic, that his goal was still the same. That's what he told himself, no matter how many times Simon's mocking voice asked that last question to him, time and again.

23

Chapter 4

Joan was breathing easier that first week, and by the weekend, and the Drayton's ball, she had firmly convinced herself that she was relieved.

However, standing by the open balcony doors, her ears blunted by the sounds of music, laughter, and wearing a newly completed white gown encrusted with pearls on the bodice, which flowed to the floor and fluttered against the matching high heeled slippers, she kept catching herself scanning bodies and faces, watching and looking for him.

It was insane. Honestly. Some sort of twisted compulsion she was sure.

Her maid had done her hair in an upsweep, which had curls crawling out around her nape, ears and forehead. She had on new silk stockings, and was conscious that since he'd told her he wanted her, she could feel her body as never before, feel textures against it in a hyper sensitive way. Whilst bathing earlier in the day, she had lain there in the tub, looking at it and realizing that it looked more sensual, sexual somehow.

Not once during her association with Robert had she felt that. That entire episode was about her pure heart and head full of dreams, about those fairy tales her mother had spun, and that alone had led her blindly to the physical, which she was positive, she had not been ready for.

She was twenty-four years old. It had made a great difference, she admitted, the years and observations, the experiences and maturing. But all of that did not mean she welcomed the fact that Lord Roger had somehow awakened her senses. She'd been attracted before; many times a handsome man, a pair of nice eyes, shoulders, or a masculine voice, they had caught her fancy. But none of that, none of them, had really stirred her.

Oh, bloody hell. As if she'd summoned him up, Joan spotted that dark figure across the room, just coming down the half-moon entry stairs. He was taller than most of the

24

men present, and for certain, he was darker. She could not help but notice the way he carried himself. It bordered on arrogance, that proud stride, and the way he moved, his jet hair reflecting the lights...it should really be a sin to possess that much charisma and masculine appeal.

He wore mostly black save the cravat. She watched him lean down to say something to an old duke in a wheeled chair, and watched the slide of that silky hair against his hard cheek, observed him straighten, smiling slightly, and pat the old man's shoulder, in a way that a completely hardened man would not have.

Joan's hands squeezed her fan a bit tighter while he moved on until he was across from her. A swirl of dancers passing between them and a wide expanse of marble floor, yet she knew the moment he saw her.

She should turn and walk outside to the balcony. She should return to the sidelines and accept dances. But she stood there for the longest time, letting her eyes fill with the image of him leaning against that column so casually. Why did she have to notice his muscular legs filled out those snug trousers better than any other man there? When he crossed his arms the evening jacket parted back to show a taut waist before gradually expanding up that broad chest, and why did she have to compare his swarthy skin and coal black hair, his chiseled face to every pasty-faced, ruddy-cheeked fellow in attendance?

Truly aggravated with herself, Joan returned to the seating, but soon after accepted a dozen dances. She focused on her partner and did not look in Roger's direction once.

Since these bloody balls went on forever, and she'd discovered that debs would torture their feet by dancing the soles out of their slippers, Joan had found her own way of easing the ache in her arches, and slipped off through one of the side entries, just by the card-room, to sit down rather heavily on a backless bench, and slip off her high-heeled pumps.

Staring out the window at the formal garden lit up from the tall windows and absently appreciating the sparkling water spraying from a center fountain, she reached down after sliding up her hem, and massaged her feet. She felt obliged to hang about until the wee hours, not because she was husband-hunting or trying to rub elbows, she was trying to honor Uncle Willy's request, and then she could go home and get on with real life.

Roger had stepped in the dark room, and leaned against the square column that sectioned off his lordship's hunting trophies from the rest of the library. He crossed his arms, eyeing that figure sitting in the spill of soft moonbeams from the massive window. His eyes scanned over the glints in her hair, curls mussed, and unlike the debs and sticklers, she did not run to repair them, so they were wispy, whimsical, around her head. Her skin was a dark cream, much more exposed to sun, he'd discovered.

And her profile, still not perfect, was nonetheless striking. She had a graceful neck. He traced that visually down to the low, stiff, pearl-encrusted bodice that exposed enough skin to make the plump tops of her breasts rival the beads in shimmer. The gown was two layers, a sheer over-layer in some iridescent cloth and a silk under-layer that was now slid up a good foot.

Speaking of feet, he could see hers encased in white silk stockings and most of her well-shaped calves. He enjoyed the moments she leaned down to rub her arches, and gave him a moon kissed view into that bodice.

He was rather surprised to find the scene so stirring. The decorated, high-heeled pumps sitting on the hardwood floor, one having fallen over, and the way she braced her hand out from her hip on the padded bench when she leaned over. It was evocative, artless, seductive, in an unintentional way, a still life of a woman in repose.

Here the music was muted, and beyond that arch of light, there were only shadows of the objects in the room. For some reason his thoughts were mocking him, trying to remind him of explicit times, dozens of nude women in all sorts of poses. His graphic mental pictures, culled from years of experience, didn't banish one sensual emotion he felt standing there looking at Joan.

Joan was in the process of settling both feet on the floor, when the hair on her arms rose. She automatically turned her head toward the entrance.

There was no mistaking that tall musculature, no matter how shadowed he was.

She braced both hands by her hips, stretching her feet out, and looking in his direction a long time. Her heartbeat sped to a hard, steady thud. He pulled away and walked toward her.

She heard the air push out of her nostrils when he stopped, a mere inch from the square of moonlight, then he was turning to lean his back against the massive bookshelves and prop the sole of his boot on the wood panels. Hands tucked in his pockets, he was visible to her in that distinct way, where she could see every feature, see the lustrous black of his eyes and hair, and detect the hollows in his face as well as that scar...

But her eyes lingered too long on the curve of his sensual mouth before she raised them, feeling an all over awareness, a strange sense of her skin while distantly aware that her heart was thundering her blood too fast through her veins.

His raspy husk, too dark and too seductive, reached her, "Do you feel beautiful sitting there in the moonlight, Joan?"

She swallowed. "No..."

"You look very...enticing...very feminine and seductive..."

She sat up slowly, now self-conscious at her previous leaned-back posture.

"Raise your skirts, sweet. At least let me look at you."

The skin of her face heated. She was whispering too. "Roger, please..."

He made a sound in his throat. "I would please us both. I would erase the memories of your girlish experience. With my mouth, my hands. Oh, Joan, you have no idea what our bodies could feel together... Uncovered...skin to skin...hot blood flowing, and senses sharp, open."

Oh God. She was starting to become light-headed, and the mental pictures he put her mind, of his dark body, her creamy one. Rubbing against each other.

She murmured, "I've no doubt your reputation is well earned..."

"Joan," he chided softly. "You speak so freely of intimacy, and yet, you fight it. There's no one here but you and I...I am thinking, speaking of you, and how I want to touch you. How I can see those silken hands, and imagine you touching me."

She shuddered and closed her eyes, wanting to flee, yet rooted to the spot by his dark, smooth whispers, helpless to the fires stirring in her blood. She wasn't a girl anymore, she was a grown woman, and he was too much man, too male an animal, for her *not* to respond. There was an odd sense of safety in the darkness, in the foot of distance, and the fact that he was here with her. As if the forbidden was allowable, just for now.

"I am not up to your...level of knowledge, your ability, to have mere sex with females, Roger." She hated the strain in her whisper. "I don't deny the temptation, all right? I'm not going to tell you that you have no effect on me.

But—"

His low-pitched tone cut her off. "Then I shall take what you *will* give me. Starting now, Joan. You say that you learned something from your previous experience and I admit, that exploring the sensual is something I take pleasure from. I will give you intimacy. Is this not what you feel now?"

"Yes," she admitted.

28

"And what will you give me in return?"

She wet her lips. "I don't...I can't imagine that there is anything I have that no other wo—"

"No. We are speaking of us, now, these moments."

"I don't know what you want." She bit her lip and looked out at the fountain, experiencing an *out of body* sensation, as if her more practical self could not believe what was happening.

"This is, perhaps, not the best time or place. But, before I leave you, look at me, Joan."

She did turn her face and stare into the shadow, and see him. She stared at that intense visage. She saw his lips move when he spoke again.

"Turn around, and face me." It was said quietly.

She obeyed.

"Raise your skirts, slowly."

Joan's fingers trembled, but she kept her eyes on his face as silk slid against silk.

She raised her hem to her thighs...

"Ah, ravishing...the silk glows but your skin, warm as cream..."

Joan watched his head lean back. He was looking at her now from under his thick lashes.

"Part them..."

"I...can't," she choked.

"Just a bit, love."

Joan mentally counted to five, and then parted her legs a mere six inches, feeling a cool rush of air.

"Joan," he husked. "You are not covered?"

"No. Oh, I can't believe I'm doing this..." she said in a whispered babble, "I...I couldn't get the gown to look right with the lingerie I had bought, so I ordered more, a different sort, from a discreet shop, but they have not arrived."

There was a soft chuckle from him that seemed mingled with surprise. "Will you show more?"

"Roger. I can't, not yet." Bloody hell, she was shaking all over.

He pushed away from the shelf, standing there only moments, before turning to leave. As he did, he said, "Until next time, Joan. You were exquisite... Sensual."

Joan left shortly after, too shaken, and too upset to mingle with the crowd or dance as if nothing had happened in that back room. All the way home, in the coach, she replayed every word, every second, while Miss Avery chattered and scratched her head under her turban, going on and on about some of the gowns and jewels. And Joan didn't hear a word. She was seeing those hooded eyes, hearing that deep voice, and seeing herself doing as she had for him, wondering, as she closed her eyes and leaned her head back against the cushioned seat, if there was some part of her that wanted to be seduced.

Chapter 5

It was much too early, by London standards, to be at home. She allowed the maid to run her bath, and as soon as the girl had hung up her gown, Joan sank into the warm water. It was pungent and heady with the musky floral scent that she had concocted at home. Lying back, relaxed in the candle-lit chamber, with only the trickle of water, and an occasional sound from the open window where the sheers fluttered, she thought of the estate—her herb gardens, and flowers, the days spent lulling outside, reading or riding her gelding through the countryside...the freedom.

Joan sighed and closed her eyes, having taken her hair down and allowed the untamed curls to go where they would. In the humid water, they normally did so and she ducked under twice, smoothing them back from her face. Eventually she bathed, again aware of her skin and the color, the texture. She patted herself dry, pulling on a garment that made her smile in whimsical memory.

When she was a tiny girl, she oft had a taste for the gothic. Between exploring old churches and castles, and hearing stories from the locals, she'd often frightened herself so severely, that she would creep to her parents' chamber and wiggle between them in the night.

When she'd grown a few years her father had a garment fashioned for her, telling her that it was a magic mantle, of sorts, that protected her from harm.

In her teen years, becoming more mature, she'd given up such fancy, but after the year with Robert she'd had a similar gown sewn, for comfort she supposed. To remember the closeness of those days when her father was the hero in her life, and to remind her that there still existed men who were capable of love and of caring about her. It was simple cotton and plain in the extreme with a scoop neck, no sleeves, and buttons down the front. It fell to her bare feet and felt like nothing next to her skin. She touched it now, smoothing it over her stomach and wondering at the stages in a woman's life. Wondering at the layers too, that sometimes did not surface or went unexplored unless some event or person drew them to the surface. She had a sudden mental picture of her mother, and recalled the maturity, the wisdom, the mysterious knowing in Anna's eyes. It made her wonder if her mother's journey had been similar. Had Anna the child, the teen, the woman, the mother, kept discovering things about herself until she had died, much too soon?

Joan was in her adjoining room when the maid and footmen came up to clear away the tub. Thinking of her servants at home, their ready smiles and cheerful openness, and the relaxed manner in which the old estate was run, Joan thanked God her parents had been as they were. She knew her servants there, their wives and children, their sorrows and joys. She reasoned that was why she'd never missed having siblings. She had always been around warm and caring people of all ages. She shook her head laughing at herself for becoming maudlin and gloomy. She was *not* lonely, and she was *not* unfilled, it was just that the more formal world here did not allow for closeness. They were not at all pleased when she admonished them to not use her title. It reminded her too much of expectations, of the ton's pressures to act and be and do as they dictated. To be something other than a real woman with an entirely different background than most of the debs here. It made her feel like a fake, a person who thought herself superior, and she did not. She simply wanted to be the woman her parents had taken such care to nurture.

"Will that be all, Miss?"

"Yes. Goodnight, Margaret." Joan glanced over from looking down at the ivy wall separating her rented house from its neighbor.

"Very good night, Miss." The maid curtsied and left.

Joan knew her neighbors in the county, as spread out as they were. She had no idea who lived in the house beside her here, these residences were rented out, several times a year, and in this neighborhood, could be a rich merchant or a middle-aged couple of the ton.

She placed Roger mentally in some gothic castle, and snorted at her own fancy. In all the rumors surrounding him, she was aware that the Earl of Wythe had the typical rich townhouse, and several estates scattered about, a hunting box in Scotland and a yacht. She'd heard little of what he did in the off season, most of the rags and papers having built his rep from his town slumming and string of affairs and lady birds.

Joan grunted. Whatever game she had allowed herself to participate in, she was in dangerous territory. He was older and far more worldly than herself, in spite of her experience. There was something about him that was primal, untamed, something powerful that warned her, when she stepped over that line, he was going to open a door to a world where he was master, and she...a...well, she may as well be a virgin, because whatever he did, speak, look, touch, it was compelling. A lure into a realm of the forbidden.

~

Over the following weeks, Joan spied Lord Wythe at the usual amusements. He was absent the ballroom, but present in the cardrooms most often. She saw him at the theater with Simon, who looked half-sotted and half-asleep through most of the play. Roger, she expected, did not do teas and musicals, but he was a regular in the park.

On Friday, she was on Bond Street with her maid, and spied him standing outside a tobacco shop, speaking with three men, one with silver hair and a roguish smile, a recently snagged confirmed bachelor, if memory served, and a rake from way back, whom it was rumored could not be reformed.

Their masculine laughter reached her where she sipped her tea at the café. Joan had her hair up and a new green and black hat atop it, with a half net of black that matched her net gloves. The day was overcast, but she'd forgone the usual calf-length jacket and wore a quarter sleeved, jade-green walking dress. She made some concessions to fashion, but refused to overdress in mild weather simply because it might rain. Still she was amused at herself, at the way she seemed to take stock of her wardrobe when Roger was within seeing distance, a rather vain habit she was developing. She mentally mocked herself for caring about the least detail and wondering why it mattered a damn, when what the man wanted to see what was under it, not if it was the height of fashion.

The street was busy, the shops bustling, and filled with debs still picking up wardrobes, and not a few brides were with their parties, flittering from shop to shop buying their trousseau.

Joan's gaze moved to her maid. She raised her brow, following Margaret's intense stare, to see several men, dressed in homespun and derbies, unloading a wagon. Amused, for they had their sleeves rolled up to their brawny forearms and muscles were bulging all over as they hefted barrels, crates and cases. She left Margaret to her entertainment and peeked back at the shop to find Roger and Simon there.

Simon nodded toward her.

She nodded back, her lips twitching as her cousin quickly became distracted by the swishing skirts of a group of females passing.

"It looks like rain, Miss."

Joan glanced at the maid, then at the darkening sky. She stood. "Come along, then. "

They walked to their coach and entered, Joan settling back about the time Simon showed up at the window.

"Care to take us up?"

"Not at all," she said at the same time fat drops began to pound their hats.

Simon spoke to the driver, and in seconds Roger was in front of her, and Simon beside him, after the maid took the seat beside her. There were shouts and squalls from the street, and much dashing across, into shops and coaches.

Whilst the driver maneuvered through the chaos, Simon supplied, "I gave Roger a lift but then loaned my coach to Smithfield, whose vehicle collided with a dray wagon. You just missed the accident."

"It's not a problem, Simon." She watched him tuck his long hair behind his ears. "Did you give the driver your address?"

"No, Roger's. We're to dine at the club tonight."

Her eyes went to Roger, who had removed his hat, and seemed to be ignoring the spray of rain on his arm as he rested it on the open window. She'd let her own flap down to prevent getting wet, but she reminded herself that he'd captained a ship at one time. She ruthlessly squashed down an image of him standing at the helm, raven hair wind-blown and his clothing wet from the ocean's spray. Yes indeed, no such image was going to be allowed to surface right now. Not whilst she could see him, smell him, almost touch him.

As if sensing her scrutiny, his dark eyes turned from looking out, watching the scramble, to her own.

She resisted flushing from the familiarity of that look, and asked, "Which estate do you retire to, on the off season?"

"I spend much of my time sailing. I still have a ship that is captained by an old friend. I am as apt to go on his runs, as I am to spend time at any of the estates."

"You don't have a favorite?" She looked at Simon. "My cousin likes the one he has in Surrey. He has a racing track there, where he can try and break his fool neck putting his bloods against the best in the county."

Simon merely grinned at her and snorted.

35

"I've been there." Roger drew her attention. "All the estates are the same in my case. Lavish and befitting the earldom, but if I had to choose, I would spend my time in Bristol."

Joan's eyes narrowed in thought. "I know it well, and I have never heard mention of your residence there."

His smile was crooked. "It used to be an old church. Since I gathered some interesting items on my travels, none of them fit with the décor of my other estates, so on a whim, I purchased an abbey they were going to tear down."

"Which is it?"

"Black cross."

She grinned and looked away.

"I see you are as amused as the ton would be, the devil earl residing on hollowed ground." His tone was dry.

"Not at all." She looked at him. "I was..." *well she could not admit she'd pictured him in such a setting*. She knew Black Cross, with its spires and arches and interesting grounds. "I played there as a child. Scared myself witless many times imagining it haunted."

His mouth curved. His dark eyes held hers. "I often feel the spirits of the dead around me there."

"How morbid." Simon yawned. "Rog, I beg you. Do not further your dark reputation by such rot. Look at the maid's face. Oh hell, I think she's fainted."

Joan glanced at the maid who opened her eyes wide, then swiftly flushed, crossed herself, and looked out the window.

"That was too bad of you," she told Roger. "Spirits indeed. 'Tis likely mice and bats in that old place."

"Yes." He shrugged. "Have you ever been inside?"

"No. Just to the main courtyard."

"You must let me know when you are home...I'll give you a tour."

Her brow rose. "Do you think I won't accept?" She laughed. "I have itched to see those chambers for many years. My father was fascinated by it too. Is it true there are dungeons and catacombs below?"

"Yes. A massive pool of dark waters, a cistern likely, in the lower chambers and many old secret passages. Though I've not explored it much myself."

"We are here," Simon said.

Joan noticed that he alighted first, and did not miss the fact that Roger's hand brushed her skirts when he stepped down. He paused, with his hand on the door after closing it, and murmured for her ears only, "Do you attend the Radford's party tonight?'

"No. I am going to Lady Greenfeld's for supper and then attending a play."

"At Covent Gardens?"

"Yes."

He gave her a long look and then nodded.

Chapter 6

She was on edge all through the wonderful dinner. The conversation at Lady Greenfeld's tended to be political, since her husband was knee deep in it. Normally such a night would be welcome after insipid teas and the normal on dits one endured at balls and musicals. But that look Roger gave her had Joan distracted throughout.

By the time she left and went home to change, she was so tense that the maid had to speak to her five times to get her attention.

"I'm sorry, Margaret, what did you ask?"

"The black cape, Miss. It must still be in the laundry. If you'll wait, I—"

"No. No just give me the one I ordered for the Masque ball next week. The emerald silk."

Joan had changed into a deep wine red gown with webbed lace overskirt. Jet beads were on the bodice and matched her shoes. She wore a simple choker of jet, which came from some ancestor she could not recall, and waited for Margaret to do the last hook on the side of her gown before she accepted the cape. She left her hair in the style it had been done for dinner—simple with combs holding it up. Joan smoothed the elbow length gloves and then hurried below where Miss Avery was waiting.

The woman was not old, only forty, but she had one of those plain faces, and for some reason, dressed in a depressing gray, often covering her head with turbans and caps. Joan suspected she read all night, or did something that kept her up late, for she fell asleep quicker than anyone she knew. She smiled at the woman though, knowing that a companion more diligent would have gotten on her nerves and under her skin rather quickly. She had no intention of allowing someone to dictate rules and stifle her, she knew how to play society's game and she was too old to need a nanny. All of which made her suspect that Uncle Willy knew her better than she suspected and likely had his spies on the estate since they used many of the same solicitors and such. And the old dear was aware she was no featherhead.

Dusk had settled. The gaslights glowed on their excursion to the theater. Still distracted, Joan attempted to use the typical scenery and traffic to divert her, but it didn't. Somewhere along the way, she had to admit that she was willingly standing on the edge of an affair, even if she wasn't having a full blown one.

Nothing lingered in her mind the way Roger's face and voice did, and nothing seemed to be able to put her body back in storage, where she'd kept it so long. She had that *each step bringing her closer, there was no going back* sort of feeling. Roger very well may, and likely was, deliberately and knowingly leading her into seduction, yet her mind was accepting it, anticipating it; on some level that shocked her more rational self. And induced her to have these mental conversations that made little difference once she was around him.

His words made her feel womanly, maybe not beautiful, she was too honest to lie to herself, but there was something beautiful in the feeling itself, something that was organic and elemental and inborn. He'd said ravishing, that last time, and the way that made her feel was indescribable.

Joan shook her head and sighed. *There were some dreams you always wanted to revisit, recapture when awake. And, this felt like a dream.* It was as if when she dreamed and her guard was down, her mind and body opened and her subconscious roamed free. Dreams were safe, they weren't something she had to deal with when awake; they weren't going to cross over into her normal life.

The coachman's deep voice jerked her out of her thoughts. She was ready when the young footman opened the coach door, glancing at Miss Avery, who seemed to be trying to see everything, the crowds and lights, at once.

Joan leaned down the few inches difference in their height, and told her, "We will sit in Viscount Berrenger's box."

Miss Avery nodded and seemed to snap to attention. Soon they were settled in Simon's box.

Joan's attention wandered during the farce, the audience as loud as the foolishness on stage, yelling and calling to the actors. She scanned the shifting crowds, noted those who slipped out, and thought she spied Simon with a fashionable impure wearing rather tall plumes in her hair and rubies the size of goose eggs. *Simon,* she sighed mentally shaking her head, the man did give her uncle fits and tried so very hard to earn his rakehell rep.

As expected, Miss Avery was snoring open-mouthed, beside her, by the second act. Joan grunted and moved her gaze away from the woman whose head was at an uncomfortable angle while she slept. Joan was, however, jerking her gaze back in the direction of the entry rather swiftly.

Roger had arrived.

He had removed his cape and hat, and was dressed quite casually in a black jacket, trousers, and boots - and a stark white shirt. His cravat was a small one, dark, blood-red with an onyx stud. She gathered that he had spent the evening at cards and brandy with Simon at the club, then proceeded straight here.

It affected her, looking at him. She noted his hair tucked behind his right ear with a strand falling free over his temple, not the complete disarray Simon was usually in, but still, the effect was stirring, drawing attention to those winged brows and that strong forehead.

Lord Wythe was visually scanning rows. When he saw her, he moved forward.

Joan's breath held until he sat down behind her.

There was no attending the play after that. His scent—leather, night wind, tobacco, man—wrapped around her like warm fingers, putting her body in high alert and ultra perception. There may as well have not been anyone else around, for he commanded every sense and awareness.

When he leaned up to whisper in her ear, chills skittered down her spine. His warm breath fanned her cheek.

"Will you walk in the gardens?"

She closed her eyes, giving herself a moment of sanity before she nodded and stood.

Miss Avery slept on.

Joan made her way out, conscious of Roger's large presence behind her, unable to keep a tremble out of her legs.

Famous for trysts, the footpaths were well populated with cloaked figures and dark shapes melting off toward the greenery. She walked slowly, deliberately trying to gather herself and to calm her swift-beating heart. Feeling a breeze on her face, and Roger's shoulder brushing hers, aware of the thin mantle fluttering back from her dress, she reached up to undo the ties that rubbed against her choker, wondering dryly why *clothing seemed suffocating suddenly.* She stopped after being sure they were completely secluded from prying eyes. Blowing out several calming breaths.

Roger was in front of her, close enough to be touching. He did not.

Her chin titled up so that she could see his eyes. They were touching her, yes, going over her as if he wished to miss nothing.

"A beautiful gown..."

"Thank you." She wet her lips, feeling his body heat, knowing that calming breath didn't help, but simply filled her lungs with his scent.

"It's very difficult. Not to kiss you, touch you."

She wanted to kiss him too. *There, an honest thought at last.* But she was also afraid that if she did, there would be no stopping. Joan had sensed before, the chemistry between them, and at this moment, it was thick, palatable, and intense. If he put that velvet mouth on hers, if he touched her in any intimate way, she was going to lose complete control.

"Your eyes tell your thoughts, Joan."

"Do they?"

"Yes," Roger husked. "Tell me."

"Speak the obvious, you mean." She laughed, breathless.

He studied her features, looked into her eyes awhile before saying, "Looking, talking...whispering... Those are the boundaries you've given me."

Joan swallowed and wondered that his jet eyes were so hard to read, too deep to fathom his real thoughts. "I'm sorry. I don't know what we're doing. I—I don't know what you're getting from this..."

"The same thing you are," he murmured softly. "Your heartbeat gets deeper, more fierce, pounding so loud that you hear it, and your skin warms, your body starts to feel alive, blood races under your skin, and your sense of smell, all of your senses, expand."

"I see." She cut him off before her knees could buckle from the sheer knowledge that *she* made him feel all of those things he was doing to her.

She scraped her teeth over her bottom lip and admitted, "Yes. That's what I feel. I do want to kiss you. I want to taste—" She stopped, thinking, *yes, oh God, I want to taste him again.* Yet Joan admitted next, "I don't want to lose control and regret..."

She sighed a shaky breath. "I've felt attractions before. Even that...my foolish, youthful mistake...I felt it. But the actual physical was not what I expected. He was selfish, and I could sense myself getting more and more distant, and my body was shutting down, instead of burning deeper."

Roger cut in. "It makes perfect sense, if you weren't getting anything from it. Even men feel used at times,

Joan. Many men will tire of a mistress, because as much as many of them pay to have a woman serving their, appetite, most *know* that they are paying highly for it. Anyone who has a sexual affair, knows the feeling of being used in some manner."

"It's not just that," Joan said softly. "I don't want to be the fool in this. I'm torn frankly, because I know what I'm going home to, and as much as I love my life and my freedom, I've never been this close to consciously doing the forbidden, not since learning those lessons. Some part of me wants this, craves it, and yes, it has everything to do with you, and we both know, to you, it is one more experience, one more game."

Roger did lift his hand and barely touch her lips with his fingertips. His eyes shimmering dark as he husked, "I openly pursued you before, Joan. And you rejected me. My stupidity I suppose. And my arrogance, for offering a public affair with such as yourself. But no one knows about this. No one but you and I."

One of his fingertips trailed down her chin. Further, to her neck, stopping just at the hollow of her throat. "I will let you in on a little secret." His lips curved and his lashes dipped. "I do not habitually keep a string of mistresses. The only woman I regularly support is close to my age, and I brought her to England many years past, a widow, penniless though quite educated. We ceased being intimate many years ago. I rarely pay for sex, Joan. But I have no qualms doing so, if I want it badly enough."

"That's hardly a secret."

He smiled softly. "Yes, I've had scores of women. A man my age with a normal appetite does, and if it is available, we take it. But what you and I are doing Joan. This, right now...never."

That admission gave her pause. "What are we doing, Roger?"

He held her gaze whilst his finger inched down to rest between her breast. "We are seducing each other..."

Joan felt the string of fire left by his touch, felt that light stroke on the inner curve of her breast. Her mind was starting to fog a bit from the stirrings in her body. "For how long...I mean, until...what?"

His gaze pinned hers. "For however long you wish, wherever you wish."

She glanced down at his dark hand, at that finger against the tender skin of her breast. Perhaps because she was watching he slowly moved it and traced the top of both mounds, the inch that was exposed.

Though the nearest gaslight was a yard away, they could both see the chill bumps spread on her skin. And the way he touched, Joan knew without a doubt he wanted to touch more. When he dropped his hand, she kept her head bowed a moment, gathering herself. Her nipples were rigid, firm against the bodice, and she did not have to stretch to imagine that finger tracing them too.

Joan raised her head. He'd stepped back a space. She was watching him while he lit a cheroot and half sat on the stone wall. That soft, warm breeze fluttered her cloak, but brought the aroma of his cheroot, and scent of him, to her. There was no escaping that chemistry, she realized, when he was near by.

"Come here."

She sighed and walked the two feet to him, and noticed right away, that his posture on the low wall put their height even.

Roger urged her forward until she stood between his knees.

Face to face, they looked deep into each other's eyes for long moments, Joan realizing that being the focus of his stare, being the cause of that heat in it, was as stimulating as if he were touching her.

He told her huskily, "You smell of night flowers."

She parted her lips, wet them, her breathing deeper, more laborious.

44

Lashes at half-mast, he whispered. "You want to touch me. You want to, Joan."

"Yes." She barely got that out.

He looked right at her. "Then touch me."

She raised her fingers, first to his broad forehead, caressing his dusky skin, liking the feel. Then she was tracing his brow, marking a path to the hollow of his cheek. Keeping her gaze on his, Joan let the pad of her fingers outline his strong nose...finally, the velvet, sensual lips.

A harsher exhalation sounded from her lungs. She mapped his lips, tracing the curve of the upper one, the slight fullness in the lower. When he parted them slightly, she swallowed, and had to look down from gazing at him, to see herself actually touching a man's mouth, *Roger's mouth,* and she was looking when his white teeth captured the tip of her middle finger gently.

Joan's eyes flew to his. His tongue touched it in a slight stroke. Something curled hot and low in her belly. Joan was openly panting, shallow and low, when he eased up, only to shock her, by opening an inch, and sliding his lips over her finger, holding it in his hot mouth a moment, before pulling back on it with a suckling motion that contracted the muscles between her legs. He did this several times, languidly, erotically.

When her wet finger was shimmering against his mouth again, he arched his chin to drag it downward, to murmur quietly, "Have you ever seen yourself aroused?"

"No. Of course not," she whispered.

"Your eyes glisten, they widen, and then—the lids look almost heavy. Your lips part just imperceptibly and that pulse in your throat quickens. It's an equally arousing picture for me."

She raised her hand to touch the cool silk of his midnight hair, hearing herself speak yet wrapped in the spell of their intimacy. "You've seen yourself...that way?"

"No. Unlike your old flame, I'm normally focused on the woman." He smiled slightly.

Her brow rose. She looked at him again. "I've no idea what is real on your face right now, and what is practiced. A rake, I have heard, is very good at this."

Roger didn't correct her, instead, he took her hand and very deliberately laid it palm flat, against his rock hard manhood. "Even I cannot fake that." He let go of her hand, holding her gaze.

She waited a moment before moving it, feeling the heat and shape of him, indeed the steel hardness before removing her hand.

"Did your lingerie arrive?"

Joan let out an abrupt breath and laughed. "Yes."

His brow arched and he murmured, "Still, scanty I hope?"

"Terrible man," she chided, smiling at his unrepentant private questions. "Yes, out of fashion necessity, they are."

"Mmm." He leaned back and to the side. Drawing from his cheroot before tossing it, he said again, "It's very difficult not to touch you." Looking her over in a way that felt very much like a deliberate caress, he said, "We need a more private place, Joan…"

She stilled. "For what…?"

"Whatever." He fingered the overskirt of her gown, and murmured, "This journey to seduction is highly arousing and has endless possibilities. And, there are limits to exploring our mutual pleasure in these public places."

"I don't know…" she searched his face, feeling a tingle of fear and temptation, of desire, but having some innate sense that she would feel pleasure with him.

It was that alone, that overrode her good sense, because whatever dark games he wished to play, she knew for certain, that now, he would be discreet.

She may never in her life have another intimate relationship with a man. That floated through her head as they gazed at each other. There was no one at home she felt compelled to seriously consider. To be honest, she'd been thinking since her parents died, planning a life alone, a productive and interesting one, but still, one without a man. *Just this once*, her mind was tempting, while her body was begging for more, *just this once, Joan.*

"Trust me to arrange something." Roger cut through her thoughts.

She chewed her lip. "How?"

"I'll send a note around, a coach for you on the nights you are free."

She blinked, her brows arched. "How am I supposed to apprise you of that?"

"Is there a back garden, an alley by your house?"

"Yes."

"I'll send him, and if you do not wish to come you can send him away."

Joan grimaced. "Is that...discreet? I don't know my London servants very well. Not like the ones at Lecrox manner."

He smiled dryly. "They are servants, Joan, they know how to be blind and deaf."

She said distracted. "That's taking a big risk."

Roger shrugged and gazed at her. "If your reputation suffers, I'll marry you."

She started laughing quietly, but really laughing.

He wasn't.

She laughed until she gathered her composure. "I'm sorry, it is just that, well, I didn't expect that from...a hardened rake. Nor do I believe you'd follow through." She sighed and shook her head.

"I would."

"No, please." She was smiling. "I am well able to suffer talk, if I decide to chance it, and I don't intend to live my life amid the ton. I simply did not wish to flaunt my private af-"

"Unlike my previous, and only offer of marriage, you would not spurn my bed. Thus, I am deadly serious, m'dear. At least you are blunt, and honest, and whatever we may have to pay for this...time...between us, we are both mature enough to go into it with our eyes open."

"Meaning I would tolerate your affairs?' Joan snorted and shook her head. "No thank you."

"Meaning," he corrected softly, "we would both have our freedom. Live our lives separate, if we so choose. But marriage would satisfy the ton, and no doubt, provide us with many hours of pleasure, Joan. However, since I do not intend to take undue risks it won't come to that. I only meant to assure you, that I am called a rake, not a cad."

"What is the difference?"

His look was chiding, "I enjoy indulging myself, and whomever I am with. I'm not interested in force, manipulation, your fortune, or promising you more than what I've offered up front."

"Well," she muttered, "that is blunt."

He smiled crookedly. "You may not say so, love. But you are just as candid. Saying it or not, you've drawn the line of what I may do, and not do."

"I'm not holding out for some romantic..." she began and then stopped, simply saying, "This is not real. Other than this, we know very little of each other, Roger. Therefore, I must limit things. There's nothing typical or even sensible about being with you. When I am not, I feel like I'm walking in two worlds, this one being the dream world."

"I've vast experience with that feeling," his gaze met hers. "Only it is 90% of mine."

She absorbed that. "You chose it. The path that gained you your rep."

"It chose me. I'm not of the ton mould. What I've lost in the past, cast me in a role too. Perhaps even before that." He stopped himself and merely said, "You cannot make yourself conform, look, or even act, against the nature that shapes you."

"Well, I believe that. But I think you play up the darker image, that you distance people. Maybe even ordinary life. I'd venture to say that you go out of your way, to perpetuate the air of mystery."

He cocked his brow.

She braved on. "It hurt. It must have, to have your parents die, believing the worst. It must have hurt terribly, even if you did not love her, to have Maria spurn you. It must have hurt to come to London and find this shallow and oft-fickle society had already judged and branded you. And, as common as it is for wealth to make us acceptable, that sort of knowledge also makes us cynical. On the one hand they condemn you, but for your title and wealth they embrace and cannot afford to ostracize you. That is what you face, and 'tis likely why you keep yourself distant from everyone."

His brow had lowered. His face was very still.

She sighed and stepped back. She'd already gone this far. "People assume that a woman's heart is softer, as soft as they assume our heads are. Maybe so. Maybe, we have to understand people and it's an automatic compulsion. I had my heart broken, for the stupidest reason, over the worst sort of cad, but it hurt. I think, sometimes, men who are accused of being hard or jaded, are simply humans that have been hurt, and do not wish to replay such an experience. I understand that fully."

He only stared at her for a long moment then asked, "And what is the point of analyzing this?"

Joan retied her cape and looked at him. "No point, except, to verbalize that the shadows that make up the most of your life, do so, because you prefer the dream, to the reality."

He stared at her for several moments more, before he arose to escort her back. "You know very little about me, Joan, or my past. For now, let us leave it there."

Whilst they were passing some thick hedges Roger stopped in the shadows, and detained her with a hand on her upper arm.

Joan glanced up, just in time to see his head descending, to feel his lips settle on hers. The kiss was urgent, swift, almost punishing, whilst his hold on her arms remained tight. He eased the kiss eventually, just enough, but the swirl of his tongue remained intimate, leaving little of the space unmarked or un-tasted.

Roger ravaged the inside of her mouth, enough to bring a moan from her throat, and to leave a sexual, carnal, tang inside Gasping when he broke the kiss, she held to him a moment with her eyes closed.

Joan raised her head to find him staring down at her. She opened her mouth to say something, but he lowered his head again, this time, raking his tongue across her lower lip before he slid it inside. This kiss was completely different. It caressed and stroked, it laved, and the flat of his tongue touched the tender inside of her mouth in ways that made her knees weak, her head light. On her second moan, he ended the kiss, with a last suckle to her bottom lip, then held her against him as she gathered herself.

"Were you making a point?" Joan finally managed.

"No. Not really. We have both wanted that kiss, for a long time. Have we not, Joan?" His breath was heavy, his tone thick.

"Yes."

He lightly touched her hair and set her back. His eyes going from her wet and swollen mouth, to her own gaze. "This time I gave it. Next time..."

He left it at that. Joan didn't need him to finish. If not for the surprise, and the total newness of such a kiss, she would have taken the opportunity to taste him back...to explore her own desire.

She awoke Miss Avery after Roger had left her at the box, and made it through the last act, still tasting him in her mouth. She caught herself twice, touching her mouth, still tingling from his. There was no doubt left that Roger wanted her, nor that she wanted him, and there was no doubt as far as her body was concerned, that he could and would make her feel things she'd never experienced before.

Chapter 7

There were times during the busy hours of the next week that Joan had to be brought back to earth by those around her. She crammed her schedule full in the day hours, having no idea why, except perhaps a self-conscious effort to head off any gossip if she did misstep in the future. She made the most of each appointment and strained her nerves trying to appear perfectly normal, when she knew bloody well that she was crossing an invisible line.

One morning at the park, Simon caught up with her, looking as if he'd spent the night in a bottle of brandy.

"Are you still angry with me, puss?"

She looked at him. "No, of course not." She shook her head at his appearance. "You look horrible, Simon. Why on earth do you drink to that point?"

He blinked against the weak sun and muttered, "Boredom. Even gambling is beginning to lose its appeal."

"I'm sure a new mistress will fix that."

He grunted. "A man hangs about town long enough, there is nothing, or no one, new."

"Then perhaps you ought to try a serious relationship."

He snorted. "With the empty-headed gaggle of debs?"

"Uncle Willy would love to have grandchildren."

"You are evil." He stared at her smile. "To wish me upon some poor woman."

"No actually, I'd feel sorry for her. But everyone comes to a point where the same old amusements are not amusing."

"No. It is just this blasted season. I am beginning to look forward to the off season. At least the faces are different."

Joan snorted. "You've always been restless, Cousin. I suppose that makes for a good rake however."

He'd been rubbing his aching head and said, "I think, I must have got into a brawl. I feel a knot on my head"

Joan chuckled. "Poor, Simon. 'Tis more like you passed out, and the footmen let you land where you would."

His mouth twisted sourly. "I miss your father, by the way."

Joan lost her smile and sighed. She missed both her parents. "So do I."

"He was disgustingly positive of course, always laughing."

She nodded. "That's because he was in love with my mother."

"Hmm." He grunted.

Joan scolded, "Love is not a disease, Cousin."

"No, just rare enough, illusive enough, so that too many other things are mistaken for it."

"Meaning girlish romance?"

"Lust, normal base desires, and so on." He nodded. "Not a subject good for my digestion."

"The problem with your belly is likely sour whiskey."

He laughed a bit, looked her over a long time, and then mused, "Why can't other women be like you, puss?"

Joan grinned. "You mean blunt and not apt to flatter your ego or…"

"Yes. I mean plain spoken."

"I'm far from perfect." She was thinking of Roger. "More flaws than assets."

His mount stumbled and he groaned and stopped.

"Goodness, you do have a head." She laughed seeing his white face. "You should be home coddling yourself."

"I'm going. I wanted to check up on you. M'father don't ask much, nor expect more than the worst from me. But he does require I keep up with your doings."

"Uncle Willy is very sweet, and he dotes on you. I will jot him a letter; thus far, I'm doing acceptable. I get a respectable amount of invites, but I am not here to make friends. I go to suppers regularly where I find the hostess pleasant and warm. I've yet to be cut direct though I'm sure my country manners and sometimes blunt speaking gives pause to the old sticklers."

"Good." He eyed her before turning his mount to leave. "No trouble from 'ole Rog then?"

She made herself remain impassive. "We understand each other much better."

He nodded, groaned again, "Bloody hell, my head feels like a cannon exploded in it." He leaned over and bussed her cheek, then rode off cursing every movement of the beast.

Joan chewed her lip watching him disappear and mindful that she was going to tell more lies, be more evasive, and have to be on her toes in the future.

She turned her own mount toward the entry, unable to worry about anything but that inevitable summons from Roger.

~

The first night that the coach appeared around back, Joan could feel her knees shaking. Having returned from a small party, she'd just finished her bath and her hair was still damp.

Drat!

Margaret was abed, and the only servant stirring was cook, whom she'd spied in the brick kitchens reading some heavy tome on Dutch cooking and muttering while trying to translate it to French.

Joan stood several moments suspended between confusion and panic, before she whipped off her gown, and hurried to the wardrobe. Pulling on a white gauzy walking skirt, she then dashed over to don her stockings and raced around buttoning a short camisole up the front. She got her feet into a pair of plain slippers, dragged the brush through her hair, and whipped on a cloak. Her heart thudding and her mind chatting *oh God, oh God, what am I doing?*

She made it almost to the back door before the plump cook called out, "Who is there?"

"'Tis just me, Andre, I'll be out awhile. Don't wait up." She hurried through the back door, grateful that the coachman turned his head, and did not look at her when she entered the vehicle.

He sped up the street, presumably to pick up Roger. She smoothed her wild hair and groaned, thinking back on that year with Robert and all the care she'd taken in dress and appearance. Hours to get ready, and now—*she hadn't had time!*

The coach stopped. Joan barely got a glance at the narrow streets before Roger entered, bringing his mysterious scent and massive form to fill the interior.

He was not in formal dress either, but unlike her, it appeared he'd deliberately chosen the white shirt that was nearly sheer, with several buttons undone down his hard chest, indecently snug breeches, tucked into wine leather boots. His hair was windblown, and his black eyes were on her.

It was late enough, so that the churn of wheels and lumber of the coach was the only clamor, aside from that thick, intense silence, whilst they stared at each other.

"You're hair is wet."

She tried to tame the curls. "I had just finished my bath."

His eyes went over her. "Leave them be, I like your hair down, natural. It gives you an entirely different look from your ton image."

She dropped her hands. "It is usually shorter, has been most of my life. But Uncle Willy had fits seeing it. He made me grow it out."

"How short?"

She held her hand to her ears, smiling. "When I was a little girl, it grew rather wild and Mother could not tame it, not even with braids. I cried the first time she cut it, well, at the time I was convinced that princesses had to have long hair, and I was going to grow up to become one, and if she cut it, all hope was gone"

He smiled.

Joan finished. "But Father found this old book on elves and fairies, and he told me the truth of how princesses become princesses, and wouldn't I rather look as delightful as a fairy?" She chuckled and shook her head. "When I got older and the maids would be in tears trying to contain it, I realized that keeping it short was only practical. I attend parties, but for the most part, my life is active and it makes sense. *" Oh Christ, was she blathering or what?* Joan groaned mentally.

However he simply nodded while his gaze roamed her face. "My mother used to tell one of our maids, who was so sheepish to be covered with thousands of freckles, that they were fairy kisses."

"My father said that too." She glanced out the window. "Where are we going?"

"I've a house just outside London. Not large, but my secretary informs me the renters had left, and it is empty. I seem to recall it has a nice garden. I sent the servants on a vacation until the end of the season."

She wet her lips, eyeing his shirt. "You look, relaxed."

His smile was knowing. "Don't be afraid, Joan. We're both adults."

"I'm not frightened. It just feels, odd." She wiped her damp palms down her skirt.

He stretched his booted feet out until his legs touched the outside of hers. With one arm along the seat back, the other on the open window, he regarded her.

"You do a lot of exploring in the countryside?"

"Yes. I have all over England. We used to guest at other estates, oh, weeks at a time. Nottingham, Lincolnshire."

"So, you have a sense of adventure?"

"My father thought so. I was fascinated by the gothic, well, I have a curious mind I think."

"Umm." He smiled. "That serves us both on this occasion." He went on. "In my travels I've explored other cultures and fascinating sites. Not much in England."

"It must have been dangerous… Privateering?"

"It was. But danger is seductive in its own way."

"Were you ever tempted to return to the high seas?"

"I am daily." He smiled short. "However, the estates cannot run themselves and though I have investments in other countries, my father's tenants are used to having access to their earl."

"Ah, you do not only rake and slum?"

He laughed again. "I manage to do both. Do you run the estate alone?"

"Father's solicitor lives nearby, and I have Sir Kimball who is a sort of secretary. But the estate runs very smoothly, just as when my father was living. I visit and know my tenants. There is very little formality. It doesn't require my constant attention, but I like being involved, staying busy." She shook her head. "I confess, I do not know how these women are so content with fashion and gossip and just socializing. My mind would rot if that were all I ever thought of. I wouldn't be able to breathe in such a narrow existence."

They were silent for some time before he said, "Tell me about your lover."

"Robert?" she grimaced.

"Yes."

Joan looked down at his boots, then back up. "He was older, twenty eight to my seventeen, my very immature and protected seventeen. His family was gentry who'd come to their vacation house, to sail every summer. He was well known in the village and the city, but I didn't meet him until some outing, you know, picnic, croquet and rowing." She leaned her head back looking at him from under her lashes.

"He was a fashionable dresser and was well traveled. I began to steal away from that party of friends my age, and listen to his tales. In any event, he started to pay me special attention. Eventually my father took note of it, and Mother too, rightly so since I was an heiress, but I must confess, that word meant nothing to me. I was, until that time, a young woman surrounded by love, people who gave me freedom, confidence, but whom I know, protected me from many things."

She waited until the coach wheels rolled over a long bridge, and then went on. "He was constantly around, and the more he was, the more I was convinced I was in love with him. I had an ideal, you see? A prince from my young dreams." She smiled at her own fancy.

"And your father let him court you?"

"No. I turned from the perfect daughter into a brat. Honestly." She laughed quietly, then said, "Looking back now, I have no idea how they stood it. I slipped off, broke rules, and disobeyed their wishes for the first time in my life. As I say, he was a man of the world. He spoke right to every silly girlhood dream I had. He even convinced me that my parents' disapproval was somehow a part of the drama. And it was, the more they said no, the more desperate it seemed in my childish mind."

"And the sex?"

Joan sat up and looked out the window. "I'd been meeting him out by the stream, riding my horse there. He'd already vowed we'd marry and that he'd die without me." She shrugged. "The usual tripe that young girls believe. I liked the wanting, the kisses, and flowery words well enough. But the first time was rough—I cried for hours. Of course he was so sweet, so comforting, that I got over it."

"But?"

"But," she admitted low-voiced, "The next few times, there was less talk, less vows of love, next to no courtship, and I was confused, thinking it was love, having already defied my parents, I gave in. But I began to feel as if he were pouncing on me the moment I got there, and to be frank, he didn't take his time nor bother with many kisses. I began to feel emotionally violated in some way, that each time, my feelings were less and less involved. Meanwhile, my father had him looked into, and was trying to tell me he was after my virtue and my fortune. But I'd gone so far, and risked everything for him, that I did not wish to believe I could have been such a fool." She added tighter, "I had trapped myself, and my pride would not let me relent, even though I felt horror at how far I'd gone..."

"He was much older, Joan. Knew the game inside and out. There are lords and rakes alike, who do that and more. Bets fly during the season on some deb's virtue, and fortune hunters are not choosy about how they gain them, or whom they seduce."

"I know that now. I'm thankful that my father set him up, paid him off, even that he bloodied his nose." She laughed. "It took awhile to get over the shame of causing my parents to go through that, to stop feeling like an utter fool. It took longer to talk to my mother about the sexual part, because that is not easy to do."

"I imagine not. Many young ladies find themselves wed by doing so, regardless if the man is a cad."

"Yes, Mother told me. But there could have been pregnancy too. I shudder to think how innocent and trusting I was." She glanced at him, flushing a little. "She also educated me about the sex. I was still confused, perhaps near the point where I would avoid it forever, hate it. Poor Mama, she had to tell me more than she was prepared to." Joan remembered Anna's dismay and stumbling through that long night of talking. She recalled they had talked until dawn and parted as friends, closer than mother and daughter.

"You still have doubts." He held her gaze. "Understandable, considering the man who introduced you to it." Roger's tone grew deeper. "A woman in her passion is such an erotic thing, that I can't say I understand men of his inclinations. Hunger sometimes makes us thoughtless or rash, even selfish, Joan, but there should be no point in adult sex, where one is left unsatisfied, or where one partner is doing something against their will." His lashes dipped. "There are too many ways, too many sensual things to experience, to have one partner insist on something, that the other does not enjoy."

Joan wet her lips, heated inside from his words. "It is beyond my scope of knowledge. Mother simply explained the relationship she had with my father, the love they had. The fact that they were equal in bed and out. "

He nodded, then asked curiously. "Why did you slap my face that first time?"

She laughed. "Because, we were at a bloody ball."

Roger smiled crookedly. "It should make you feel very good to know I want you. I'm not out to do as your first lover did, Joan. I would enjoy very much, seeing you revel in your sensual hungers."

Her whole body flamed anew from that voice, with that body, making *that* sound like a promise. As she stared at him, he looked very much the mysterious and dangerous seducer. She admitted, "You are very much the opposite of him."

"The dark prince…" He grinned.

"No, more the bloody pirate." She laughed softly. "Everything about you is enigmatic. You must know that, you reek of the forbidden." She sighed and murmured, "A part of me is very much drawn to that. Perhaps, I've retained some of my young fancies, because I look at you, and think of tales where your sort carry off the most ravishing beauties of the land, which I am not. I am about as ordinary as they come."

"No. You insist so. But I disagree." His eyes went over her. "As for the lure, you will find me a flesh and blood man. I expect, after we have made this trip a few times, we will both have exposed everything about ourselves."

Those ebony eyes stared deeply. "The intimacy I am giving you, is not something I have invited before, Joan. Mistresses and females for sex, are not interested in such things."

She nodded. She knew that. And it was the second time he'd reminded her just what he was doing for her benefit.

Roger assisted her out when the coachman halted before the front door. The brick house set back from the main road, and though it held its own quaint charm, it was more informal than a townhouse.

The lanterns were lit in the drive. He spoke to the coachmen, sending him to the carriage house with its own apartments to wait. A golden light flooded from inside the house. He reached above the door for the key.

When the door opened, he allowed Joan to step through, following and permitting his eyes to scan the interior. His instructions had been followed. The main room had a lit fire in the hearth; a bottle of wine and two glasses were placed on a low table. Roger deemed the main parlor comfortable for now, unpretentious, with its leather sofa and two overstuffed chairs. There were three tables, two holding vases of fresh flowers that perfumed the air subtly, and mingled with the firewood, beeswax and lemon oil.

He glanced at Joan. "Wine?"

She'd sat down on the edge of the sofa and had removed her cloak. Roger thought her eyes were a bit wide with nervousness when she nodded. He poured them both a glass and hunched down to stir the fire, giving her time to sip, and hopefully to relax, and giving himself time to think.

He'd gone through some surprising emotions since meeting this woman. There was more than his ego involved in not giving up and moving on. Her slap, her rebuff, those were things he hardly lost sleep over. As he always knew *where* to find a willing bed partner, before

Joan, he would have forgotten it as quickly as he had instigated it. At this moment there were a dozen ton addresses he could drive to and the back doors would open to him, the women, ladies of title and wealth, would invite him to their chamber. But he was here, where he most wanted to be.

Roger sat aside the poker and dusted his hands. Standing to take his wineglass and sip. She was sitting back now, looking around and up at the heavy beamed ceiling.

There was that chemistry, he thought. It built every time they were together. There was also the taste of her that had cost him a night's sleep after Covent Gardens. Gazing at her now, clothes a bit rumpled, a plain walking skirt, a camisole that buttoned down the front with ribbon shoulder straps, plain white, seductive, ordinary, yet with her mussed curls floating around her head he could not think of anything more alluring.

There was something fresh and unaffected, something open about her looks. And despite losing her virginity, there was still that aura around her, that sense of untapped, untested passion that was under the surface. There were times it showed, in her green eyes. Yes, there he could see the desire that her foolish first lover had caused her to bury, to fear. She may well do so but her body reacted to him, and when it did, her breathing, her heartbeat, it all signaled a body that was capable of full passion.

Roger wasn't sure at all what he doing, where he was headed, or why he had led them to this unusual path. She would not have an affair in the context her mind defined it. It had taken his instincts, perhaps his own hunger, to find this alternative. To his mind, an affair still. Yet for some reason she was in his constant thoughts, on his mind. And, he wanted to see where this journey took them.

Joan set her half-empty glass on the table; thus he walked over and sat in the chair facing her, resting the bottom of his glass on his thigh. He searched her face.

"Would you like to go above or are you more comfortable here?"

She met his gaze, her eyes moving over his face in return in a way that stirred him. He already realized he enjoyed the way she looked at him. He liked the want in hers, so different from other women, so real and open.

"I've no idea," she admitted stiffly. " I've told you my experience. I know nothing of these sorts of things."

He leaned forward, still holding her gaze. Their voices were quiet, hushed in the empty house. "Do you want to feel pleasure?"

She swallowed and her cheeks flushed slightly, so he dropped his pitch deeper.

"This is mutual, equal, Joan. Talk to me. Is it too soon for touches, kisses? Are you still afraid you will regret it?"

He felt like groaning when she nodded, because he'd rather be besides her, kissing her, touching her. But he was willing to enjoy the journey, whatever it entailed. He set out in the coach to relax her, and it had worked, now he knew when it was time to lead her where she really did want to go.

"Trust? Yes, you need to trust yourself as much as you will come to trust me." He looked down at the wine in his glass a moment, then back up from beneath his lashes to find her gazing at him. That look was curious enough for him to chance, "Let us begin exploring that." He set the glass down and stood reaching for her hand.

She gave it. Roger pulled her to her feet. Lighting a taper from the mantle, he then led her above and stopped at one bedchamber, before settling on the rear one with large windows, and enough moon-glow so that he could blow out the candle and still have the perfect intimate lighting.

Once more in the shadows, he walked her to the window and stood behind her, his body close enough to feel. His hands lightly on her arms.

He whispered, "Can you feel me?"

"Yes."

Roger lowered his head, breathing in her scent of woman and flowers, and whispered in her ear, "I can feel you, smell your perfume, heady, stimulating."

He let his mouth nearly touch her nape, her shoulder, wanting to lave and suckle, but only breathed heated against her skin.

"Your skin is soft, scented, and my mouth waters to taste you. Imagine how it will feel, my tongue bathing your skin, laving the hollow of your throat, the tips of your breasts."

He could feel her breathing intensify, feel that tremor run through her. He breathed against her skin again, making a sound of pleasure in his throat, and flexing his fingers on her arms. The moment she leaned her head back against him, he let his hands progress, stopping under her breasts, feeling the inflexible hammer of her heart. And feeling it echo in his own body.

"Tell me, whisper to me, Joan, tell me what you desire."

She did not, but his body flamed when her head lifted, and then her fingers went to the buttons of the camisole.

Roger was taut as stone, his face dewed with sweat when she finished unbuttoning, and pulled the edges opened, so that her tight-tipped breasts were exposed for his view.

He had to close his eyes a moment and catch his fleeting control. Then, he looked at them, their shallow roundness, the chills on her skin, the silken sheen of moonlight, and the blush-rose distended nipples making his mouth water again.

The husk was not deliberate, but rather authentic as he said, "Lovely, so sweet and tempting, they are aching for my touch, my mouth?"

She seemed to capture her breath, before she whispered strained, "They ache."

That confession sent fire through his blood. He knew how to soothe that ache, and it was doubly hard not to do it right away.

He stepped back and peeled off the camisole, slowly dragging it back over her shoulders, down her arms. Kneeling down a moment, Roger lifted her feet and removed the slippers. He arose again. Had his hands on the tapes of her skirt.

"Roger…"

He paused, hearing that nervous thread under the desire. He glanced around the room, spying the long mirror. "Come here." He walked over and slid the vanity bench in front of the mirror. Re-lighting the candle when she sat down, he placed it on the floor so that she could see her reflection clearly.

What he saw was painfully arousing, her bare torso and thrusting breasts, her flushed face amid that riot of curls, but more so, the glitter in her green eyes. Mentally he groaned. He would not let himself rush her, but it was bloody hard to do. He had never had to check himself so many times before he'd even gotten the woman in bed. This was going to take every ounce of patience he could summon. But it would be worth it he told himself. It was going to be worth waiting for. He positioned himself behind her, close to her back, and more in the shadow. He wet his lips, let his gaze run down her, saying softly, "Raise your skirts."

Joan glanced from her image, up to him, through the mirror, keeping her eyes there as she slid the skirt up to her thighs. Roger groaned, out loud this time—at the contrast between those ivory silk stockings and her bare skin, the beautiful shape of her legs, the downy hair at the tops of her thighs.

"Touch your skin…"

Her breath shook out audibly. Her eyes were closed. She ran her palms tentatively from her ankles, over the silk, to the flesh of her thighs.

65

It was mesmerizing. He glanced at her face too, to judge her reaction. She was touching her breasts, her lips were parted and when she had lowered her hands back to her thighs her teeth sank into her lip. Those lashes fluttered open. Eyes glittering she once more met his reflection.

"Do what you feel, what you wish, Joan." His voice was getting remote, deeper.

She rasped, so delicate he barely heard, "I can feel you, against my back."

His smile was strained. "Love, I'd have to be dead not to react. I don't know the details of your experience, but there's no way a man can mask his arousal."

She nodded. "I don't…mind. I just…I feel…"

He sighed heavily, mentally cursing his body, and said, "Let us get you where I am. I know how to ease the ache, for both or either of us. For now, don't think of what I may be in need of. I'm no Robert. Come as far as I have, Joan." He held her gaze. "Meet me here."

Joan looked back at her reflection in the glass, taking in the disheveled well-bred woman with glittering eyes and flushed skin. Her other half. The person he wanted to introduce her to tonight.

Roger began to whisper, to describe her in sensual and erotic terms. He found it bloody easy to do, as he was in essence, speaking what he felt. He used words, phrases that were visual, sensual, stimulating. And felt his heart race as hers did, telling him by the shorter pants that she was becoming more exited.

She arched her neck, her head nearly touching his stomach, her pose one of complete absorption and abandon whilst somewhere his thoughts became less conscious and he talked, he whispered, ardent and aroused and beyond any plan or forethought. Roger verbally made love to her, sexually lost himself in watching her body shivering, quivering, tightening, and nothing, nothing in his memory, equaled the expression on her face, the absolute surrender to the moment.

Not even in his speculation before then, could he have imagined it, imagined his reaction to it. And somewhere as he spoke, he realized that with a mere two kisses as tangible contact between them, he had not sampled the fires that were just stirring, just rising to the surface. It was igniting his body, searing the fiery words that glided past his lips, stirring his sexual lusts and driving him a little insane with craving to taste what he witnessed happening to her.

He was not calm, in fact his legs were trembling when he sat on his haunches and rested his forehead against her shoulder blades. "Love, give me a moment." His hands grasped the bench. He was talking to himself now, trying to calm down. Bloody Christ, he could not believe what this was doing to him.

~

Joan opened her eyes the moment his silken hair and warm forehead touched her naked back. It was when she felt his trembling that she made herself walk mentally far enough out of the haze to reach and cover his tense hand. He was gripping the bench edge hard.

"This is madness."

He laughed, feeble and tense. "Calm yourself, I'm merely gathering my control."

"Roger." She slid her hand up his wrist, his forearm, that was rigid with tense sinew and muscle. "Perhaps we shouldn't."

"Joan." He lifted his head, then captured her hand, holding it tightly a moment before he stood again. Their gaze met in the mirror. She could see the taut lines of his face, the struggle in his eyes.

But he murmured, "How far will you let this go?"

"I don't know." She was a jumble inside, a tangle of hunger and desire, her mind crowded with his whispers, her skin famished in some strange way. She'd never encountered this side of herself and its ability to lust-daze her.

"Perhaps I am a fool, and we should just do this, the sex, and it will be done. Over, for us both." Naturally, she was a bit frightened at the way she was feeling. She had given herself to a man before, and never, ever felt like this.

"It doesn't work that way." He smiled with effort. "Attraction tends to increase. And besides, the ultimate of which you speak takes thought, preparation, that I ignored tonight." He laughed with helpless disgust. "I, the rake, don't have a French letter."

She thanked God at least he was thinking of that! The consequences were the furthest thing from her mind at the moment. She was trying to make sense of something that made no sense. "But, do you think that is it? That we're just attracted, and once we do this—"

"I think," Roger cut her off softly, "that I have no intention of letting you regret this. You're making too much of my arousal, love. I won't die, I assure you." He smiled more clearly this time, then went on gently. "You must grow used to me this way, because, you are an exciting creature and seeing you like this, is going to affect me."

She likely sounded more innocent than she was. Joan bit her lip and laughed shakily. "Oh, Roger, what the bloody hell are we doing?"

He sighed and winked. "Enjoying ourselves. Now, stop looking at me as if I was being tortured."

She smiled too. "You look tortured."

He laughed aloud that time, and hung his head a moment, scraping his hair back, tucking it behind his ears before raising it again.

He came round in front of her, sliding the candle away and sitting on his haunches. When his warm hands rested on her thighs, above the stockings, Joan flinched at first contact, but he was focused on her face, hence she met his gaze with full knowledge that her legs were shaking. That she actually liked the feel of his touch.

"Did you feel it yet, the pleasure?"

"Yes," she admitted softly. It felt as if she were intoxicated, floating, yet hot and so very hungry.

He nodded. "The next time, Joan. You must talk to me. I'm enjoying this as much as you, in spite of what you assume. But I cannot read your mind. It would really torture me to step beyond your boundaries before you are willing and have you pull back, or at the worst, end what little you have allowed me."

She blurted again, "You can have any woman, Roger."

"Not quite, please refrain from saying that." His smile was teasing. "It has nothing to do with us. With this. Let us get beyond that. I'm here because I want to be, and so are you. Yes, I can find a willing body. If that was what I wanted, don't you think I would do so?"

"I suppose."

He returned tightly. "You know it, Joan."

She stared into his eyes. Yes, she knew it. He was here, with her, because he wanted to be doing what they were doing.

His gaze dropped to her breasts and stayed there long enough for her nipples to start burning and aching again. When he lifted them, she saw the question before he asked.

"Can I?"

"Yes." Mentally she thought, *please yes, please touch me.*

His hands on her thighs urged her further toward him. Joan murmured because her thighs had to spread for his torso to fit between and the hands that were there, slid back, under the pool of skirt, to float beneath her satin undergarment and rest on her lower hips. She hissed sharply inward watching when his tongue came out just enough and lightly flicked her nipple. It felt like liquid fire. Her legs flexed inward with instinctual response. And again, until she was containing him there with them.

He treated both tips to soft strokes of that pink muscle. Never going beyond the dark peak, till the sensations pulsating through her body were stronger than anything she'd felt before. A mass of trembles, scarcely breathing from the sensitivity, Joan nearly came off the bench when he widened his lave, moving his head, using the flat of his tongue to wet the aureole. He moved his head languidly, flattened his tongue to cover more expanse and left them shimmering and damp.

"Roger!" She arched her neck, unable to avoid the lifting of her hips; her thighs were pushing against his chest. She ached everywhere now, her entire body felt like one sexual throb. And when she thought she could not possibly feel more, his mouth opened, lips spreading, scorching over a fair section of her breast. He suckled, alternating between the tip and fitting the flesh in his mouth. He varied his suckling. His teeth smoothly raked, his tongue licked, and his lips clamped tighter and greedy.

"Oh God...I...can't...I..." she gave up and buried her hands in his hair, her head descending forward. Her stomach muscles cinched and jerked. "I can't take this," she whispered. Her eyes were open, her lips panting out harsh breaths.

When he glanced up, his sensual mouth was still locked on her nipple. Roger's eyes were shimmering with hot pleasure. The sight of it excited her further.

She whispered, honest, helpless. "I've never felt this before. I don't know what to do."

He let her nipple slip free, his lips wet, dusky. He licked them. Roger eased back enough so they were more eye to eye.

Her hands slid from his hair and gripped the bench edge.

Joan felt her heart would leap out of her chest as she became aware that his hands were moving under the hem. For a moment she was alarmed, and it must have showed from what he rasped next.

"Have you climaxed before?"

"No." She didn't have a blush in her at this point. She was simply too far gone. "I'm only vaguely aware of what it is for a woman."

He slid one hand free and pried her hand loose from the bench with a tense smile, saying huskily, "We'll do this together."

She allowed him to guide her hand, and felt his fingers over hers when they found the slit in the satin. Shocked at the heat, the sticky wetness, the soft feel of herself there, Joan whispered rushed, "Am I supposed to…"

"Yes." Something flickered in his glance and he muttered, "The bloody bastard should have made you wet before."

"I don't care about him at the moment." Her voice was tense, not so much from her own touch, but from the fact that his warm, callused finger had slipped between the lips and touched some spot that made her heart nearly cease.

"Here," he told her hoarsely, watching her face, as she was watching his. Joan was half-afraid to look down.

He'd used his fingers to guide hers to that spot. When he began to move it, so that she was stroking, causing soft friction, she knew she was about to make a fool of herself, but said, "I can't take this, Roger, I can't."

"You said that before, love," he soothed. "It's simply intense. Strong. If you sink into it, and not resist, you control it, you're going to love this."

Her lips pursed to blow out a calming breath, Joan kept her gaze on his face even when her muscles flexed, and her legs trembled so hard she thought she'd fall over. It was an odd burn, a squeezing kind of pressure that was so sexual she was amazed at it. But the bench began to creek slightly when she found it easier to rock into the touch, to move her hips and rub in counterpoint.

Joan could feel the sensations building, feel her skin tingle, tighten, swell. Her body naturally craved whatever was coming. She felt a spark of fire go through her. Her lips parted, her eyes closing a moment. *It was getting better, stronger, more intense, and harder.*

Roger leaned in and took her nipple again. She groaned and rested her forehead against his hair. Feeling each suckle push the sensation further to the extreme.

It was nothing compared to the moment his finger moved and slid deep inside her, filling that channel of hungry nerves.

Her head went back. "Oh, Roger!" she cried out, harsh sounds streaming from her throat, guttural and deep. He thrust in slowly yet deep and pulled out, back deep again, while his lips locked tight on her nipple, his suckling harder and harder. Her own touch making friction and bringing that sensation to a point of combustion.

When the climax arrived, amid her tight, guttural warning, her legs jerked in against him and her inner muscles milked his finger so hard she could feel it, but couldn't stop it. With each contraction Joan gasped. Though she'd moved her own hand away, now having tangled them in his hair, the climax extended out, because of Roger, keeping his touch buried inside.

Her musk, her sexual fragrance was potent when he released her nipple. She raised her head. Her lids were heavy, mind floating. She felt bereft the moment he stopped. But was swiftly compensated.

He was on his knees and pulled her close, letting her lie against him, letting her hold to him a moment. *It was what she needed.* It did not surprise her that he knew that. Closer than they had ever been, her arms around him, she breathed a long sigh against his throat. Knowing somewhere in her mind that she was never going to forget this moment, this feeling, or this man.

"It was magnificent, Joan." His voice rumbled in his chest.

"Yes," she whispered. "A bit overwhelming at first, but the most incredible thing." She let her lips graze his warm flesh and whispered, "Thank you."

"My pleasure." He eased back, shaking his hair back out of his eyes, and sliding his hands down until they rested on her knees. "It is late."

She nodded. "But we have time for you."

His gaze searched her expression. "Are you ready for that?"

She glanced down at the obvious distention against the snug fabric. He was so rigid that his shape and length were evident. She wasn't surprised at this point, to feel herself grow aroused again at the thought of it. Joan was looking in his eyes when she said simply, "Where and how?"

He laughed softly, a bit powerless, and stood, walking over to the shadowed bed and pulling off his shirt.

"My God," she blurted, observing the play of muscle in his back, seeing the sculpted, dusky skin for the first time. "You are magnificent, Roger."

He was, incredibly so.

He laid his shirt on the foot board, scraping his mussed hair back while he glanced at her.

Joan wet her lips, her eyes skimming over his upper arms and shoulders.

"Turn around please." Her voice caught when he did. She knew her eyes grew wider, moving from the sinew of his throat and collarbone, over each pectoral and tight-tipped male nipple, down ridges of muscle to a taut waist. She was sure there were flaws, scars, but she could only admire the obvious perfection of him. For his height and his swarthy coloring, he was an exquisite virile animal, an absolutely masculine man.

"Joan." He whispered tightly.

Her eyes raised to his. "No wonder women like to see you unclothed."

His laugh was strained again, as if he did not expect her to say such things. He leaned his head back a moment, closing his eyes. They were hot with glowing fires when he lowered them. "Thank you."

She smiled and picked up her camisole, but he stopped her from buttoning it.

Standing close to him she gazed up saying frankly, "You'll have to talk me through this."

He laid a white handkerchief somewhere back on the bed. Then, Roger sat down on the edge. This time, she was standing between his legs. He leaned back, beginning to unlatch his trousers, stopping at the merest hint of ebony curls.

"Are you sure?"

She wasn't completely, because she'd not seen Robert's manhood; everything had taken place with them half dressed. She reached out and traced the hair from his navel to his own hand. She liked the look of it, the sheen against his darkly tanned skin. "Yes."

Joan knew he was watching her face, while the rest of the covering parted. Her blood caught fire as his distended sex was completely free, smooth, silky looking yet strong, so very potent and erotic. The hue was between a deep peach and darker pink. It looked strong but velvet-sleek.

He was still slightly leaned back on his elbows, when she reached out and touched it, wrapping her fingers around it. The heat surprising her as much as the wonderful feel.

Joan fisted him just under the crown, the pulse of him beating amorously against her palm. His bigger hand covered hers, veined, fingers warmer, more callused, masculine and sure of what they were doing. He leaned back, all the way down, while his hand guided hers, up and down the length.

As wonderful as it felt, and it did, she snuck a glance at his expression, further aroused herself by the filled veins in his neck, the sight of his closed eyes, the utter sensuality of him laying there, nearly nude. She saw his stomach cinch, watched the quiver in his body even as she reveled in what their hands were doing, in what hers was feeling.

His eyes slid open, looking more like wet onyx, and sending her some unspoken message. He held her hand tight, motionless. His other brought the square of linen to his thigh.

"This is where it gets messy, love." He wet his dry lips and he gently moved her hand away.

Joan was able to guess his meaning. Consequently, when he sat up, obviously intending to finish himself, Joan smiled, easily, and moved his hand, replacing it with her own again. She husked, "Fast or slow?"

He shuddered, his expression utterly taut. his eyes searching her face. Whatever he saw made him say, "In that case…"

He moved her hand again, and urged her to the bed, thus she lay beside him. Rolling so they faced each other, Roger replaced her hand, sliding it on him with a smooth groan of pleasure.

Joan was aware that he had the linen square ready. But she was surprised, when he angled so that he could kiss her. Doing so lightly, hotly, more tongue than lips, before he whispered against her mouth, "Harder."

She firmed her grip feeling sexual heat race through her.

He kissed her again, his tongue plunging deep before he pulled out. "Faster."

She was so caught up in his kisses, the sheer hunger and rawness in them, and her breathing now matched his pace. She swallowed his low groan, as their mouths were wide, tongues thrust against each other, only vaguely aware he was shuddering in climax.

He pulled back, panting, his cheek against her forehead, his hand having replaced hers.

Instinctively she touched him, soothing his spine, lightly rubbing his chest. In her mind she understood what he felt watching her, because she'd felt it just now too, and she stroked his arm and back, feeling those tense-held muscles relaxing and feeling the relentless beat of his heart slow to normal.

He rolled to his back eventually, and she to hers. While he made repairs to his breeches, she buttoned her camisole.

It was long moments of stillness, of silence, before he said, "I must get you home."

"Yes." She stared up at the ceiling, feeling as if days had passed instead of hours. Feeling as if they had been to another world.

In a short time they were dressed, having done so with equal quiet. Below, they finished their warmed wine. He doused the fire and had her wait on the stoop while he roused the coachman.

On the trip back, she was chilled. Fog lay thick and moist over the city, rolling like smoke past the coach windows.

Roger moved and sat beside her, his arm around her. "Cold?"

"Mmm. And sleepy." She snuggled into him.

He laughed . "Perhaps we shall leave some clothing there and stay the night next time."

"Do you? Stay the night with your mistresses?"

He sighed as if he did not like the subject. "No."

She laughed. "You really must not get so angry when I mention them. It was a question spurred by curiosity."

Roger glanced down at her. "You think I am simply following the usual pattern, no matter how much I say otherwise."

"No. But, oh, all right. I won't ask again."

"Ask all you wish. But I shall keep saying, what we do, Joan, is between us, and I have not set out to follow some well laid plan."

"I believe you. I do, I just…"

He pushed her head against his shoulder and grunted, "Sleep, Joan, I'll wake you at your house."

She did sleep, but did not awaken until he was tucking her into bed.

"Are you daft!" She sat up suddenly. "You carried me in here?"

"Shhh." He grinned and pushed her rather roughly back down. "Not a soul is stirring, unless you keep screeching." He leaned down and kissed her temple.

"Goodnight, Joan."

She could only stare at him. "Be quiet when you leave."

He was. She lay there listening and on edge, but she never heard anything but the crunch when the coach passed by.

Chapter 8

Joan lingered in a hot bath the next noon, prior to dressing for a luncheon she was scheduled to attend. It was amazing she thought, by evening and on her way to another appointment, how she could be so normal and conduct life so normally, after what had passed the night before.

But she did it, and for four days she wore herself out keeping her schedule to the letter. The fifth day, she even ran into Roger, having attended a supper where he showed up late. Later in the music room, being entertained by their hostess who played the harp, she sat primly, modestly dressed in gold silk and applying her lace fan. She even glanced at him, arching her brow at his black scowl.

His dark eyes shifted beside her.

She gathered his dislike was for the Baron Templeton, whose gloved hand rested on the back of her chair. Joan rolled her eyes, and then kept them on the hostess, wondering that a rake like Lord Wythe could possibly be possessive of his women. He'd all but said differently. Besides she wasn't his woman, or any man's, and by the time the party was breaking up, she was sure she'd imagined the whole thing. She kept asking herself though, what in blazes she would do if he was that possessive type, seeing that they were pretending to *not* have an affair. It was a situation she didn't care to think about. Besides, if she thought of that, she'd have to wonder if he was faithful, and she didn't want to think of that either.

But the very next evening, at the masque ball, she kept feeling eyes on her during every dance, and did not have to guess whose they were. At first opportunity, Joan went for refreshment, rubbing an itch under her green mask and idly glancing around. Black and white were the predominate colors, a few in green like herself, but she knew she could pick him out, and did. He was bloody tall and not surprisingly standing by the balcony doors.

The punch was weak but soothing. As usual, the room was stifling hot and the air was thick with perfume, sweat, and the aroma of gardenias. She had the feeling Roger was glaring at her. She sighed and contrarily accepted two more dances before she finally headed in his direction.

People were fairly close, trying to get air, and many spread out on the lawn. He did not ask, but obviously expected her to follow when he skirted around the room and exited to the side garden.

"You've been glaring at me all evening." She got to the point, and passed by him while he lit a cheroot, seating herself on a marble bench that matched another flanking a fountain.

"Have I?" He sounded tense. He pulled his mask off and tucked it into his pocket, walking over and resting his boot sole next to her hip.

She leaned back, a smile on her lips. "And what was that look you gave poor Baron Templeton?"

"I've no idea what you mean." He met her gaze blowing smoke from his mouth.

She coughed and fanned it away from her face. "I am not such a fool as to believe you are possessive."

"Never."

"Or jealous."

"No."

"Besides I'm not one of your women."

"Are you leaving for Bristol after the last ball?"

She blinked. "Yes."

"Send word to Black Cross when you are settled and I'll give you that tour."

"Very well." She frowned. "As I was saying..."

He leaned down swiftly, and pressed his mouth to hers, spreading his lips over hers, sliding his tongue in hot and sleek.

Her word was cut off, lost, ending in a moan.

When he raised, taking his prior position, both their lips were damp.

Catching her breath, Joan watched him take several draws blowing out the smoke before she grit, "What was that about?"

He tossed the cheroot and took a flask from his pocket, taking a pull before offering it to her.

She sniffed. "Brandy?"

"Yes."

She took a small sip. "Now I wa…"

He replaced the cap still swishing some in his mouth, eyeing her in a still way that put chills up her spine.

"Roger?"

He swallowed it and ran his tongue over his lips.

Joan felt it as if he'd kissed her again. "What is wrong?"

"Not a thing."

She stood and considered him. "Are we, we will meet again before the end of the season?"

He looked at her mouth. "Tonight."

"I don't know." She eyed his face. "You seem, tense."

He smiled.

Though her loins turned liquid, she murmured, "I see." And left him there while she returned to the ballroom.

For several hours she ignored him. She had to. There was no bloody way she would consider that he was jealous, or that their association made him feel anything but *want* for her. No, she kept telling herself. She would not be a fool again. Thus far she could keep one part of her wholly separate from the other, and she planned on getting better at it. Yes. To the point that, during the night, she was not lying and thinking of him, visualizing him. She had no intention of picking up her life and being preoccupied with what she *could not* have with a rakehell like Wythe.

Resting her feet some hours later, Joan found a far corner with an open window, wincing at the needles in her toes from making herself dance past the point of warning. She'd give these Londoners their due, the debs at least;

they must have feet of leather. She gave up on the punch and managed to help herself to the duke's port, yawning and more than ready to call it a night. She'd been socializing like a mad woman this week, and losing a few needed hours of sleep thinking of Wythe.

Joan jumped slightly, catching a shadow out the corner of her eye. She sighed, muttering a curse at his spooking her when Roger walked over to stand beside her.

"You are in a better mood?"

"I wasn't in a poor one before."

She snorted and saw him look down.

"My feet hurt."

He smiled, still mask-less, apparently not caring. She could only be thankful for the distance of the crowd when he turned as if looking at the window, their sides overlapping by inches and said, "I want to touch you."

Joan drank the rest of the port, her eyes blindly ahead. "Now?"

He did something, made a sound like a groan and nudged her to the point she walked back several feet.

"Roger…this…not…"

He half sat in the window. "Stand in front of me," he husked.

"Oh, not here."

But he pulled the drape to the enclosure half shut, masking them from the crowd. The dark space filled with quick, hot breathing after he kissed her explicitly and then muttered, "I want to taste you."

"I think you have," she swallowed.

"No." He bit her ear, then cupped her through her gown. "This."

Joan groaned and hated to remind him, because her blood was now aflame, "We are likely moving the drapes."

He grunted, and then with a vulgar curse pulled it back.

She stepped several feet away, feeling the heat in her face, and suddenly hungry for him. Her bloody legs barely held her up. She cast him a stark glance as he stood there beside her. Distance did not lessen the tension, nor the like hunger she sensed in him.

He was right, it simply amplified. In fact, it was taking up more of her thoughts than she wanted it to.

Look at him, Joan thought...*He is the epitome of rakehell, I must be out of my bloody mind.*

But oh, when he kissed her, touched her, when he said...it just occurred to her what he'd said! She jerked her gaze away, staring at the crowd. *That* was beyond the boundary. It was downright shocking.

"I'm leaving." She spared him a glance as she took a step.

"We'll meet."

"No." She kept walking, and didn't stop until she'd awakened Miss Avery. In moments she was on her way home. But after her bath, she did not sleep, as tired as she was, she lay there tensely waiting for the sound of that bloody coach.

It did not come. He wanted to taste her, there! She slid down and pulled the cover over her head groaning. The man was tying her up in knots.

Chapter 9

Somewhere near dawn, she slept from sheer exhaustion. Joan did not arise until early evening, sitting on the bed after her bath, having no desire to go anywhere.

Finally she dragged herself out for an evening ride in the park. Thinking to clear her head, she had her ride and kept the mare at a sedate walk while she tried to decide if the sensible part of her should override all else and go back home early, or if that one night was so, *fantastic*, that she was just stupid enough to believe she could have a few more and then end it.

"Bloody hell." She paused under some trees. Her hat itched, the combs in her hair hurt. She was getting herself into one of those irritable moods that was sure to bring on a full-blown headache. She'd never felt this bloody stuff before Roger. Who knew that climaxing would suddenly open the flood gates to all of her hungers and put her in a state of constant, high arousal, for him. Just for him.

When Wythe galloped up on his muscled stallion, Joan set her teeth and rolled her eyes. *It was too unfair.* She was supposed to resist temptation when he was right in her face? Hadn't that been how it all started?

His mount nudged hers. He looked at her, taking his time doing so. His hair windblown. Absent a cravat and hat, wearing all black except for a ruffled shirt that had two buttons undone.

"I thought you'd left."

"The park?"

"No, the city." His gaze scanned her face.

"I've been considering it...leaving early."

"Why?"

"Because," she sighed. "I am sane a few moments of the day. And, when I am, I have to question what the bloody hell I'm doing playing games with a man like you."

He captured her gaze. "Being pleasured."

He just had to say that. Joan moaned in her mind.

"Only once, and you are ready to call it quits?"

"It went pretty far, Roger."

"We've only begun."

She saw the promise, the sensual intent in his eyes. "I'm not coming back next season, and unlike London, I know everyone in Bristol."

He considered her for a long time, then murmured, "Come tonight, and then decide. If you still feel the same…" He nodded and rode off.

She sat awhile between screaming and tears in her sexual tension and mental battle before heading home, choking down a dinner, then retiring to her room. This time, she was dressed when the coach came. She wore a peach gown with a long skirted jacket and again, did not put her hair up. She could have been in rags as far as her body was concerned.

Roger was dressed as casual as before. But unlike the last time, he wasn't up to talk, and sat beside her, then pulled down the window flaps and took her in his arms.

Her palms cupping his cheeks, Joan was aware of sliding down in the seat, of his bigger, warmer body, half covering her. He raised an inch to let her breathe. She stared at his tense visage.

His free hand was raising her skirts, sliding up the inside of her thigh, and finding her uncovered.

"This is the last time," she husked, making a sound in her throat as he found her damp heat. Her body grew wetter at his touch, the flames sparking higher and the fog already starting in her head.

He lowered his head, running his tongue over her lips in an explicit, sensual manner, and then kissing her deeply and slowly.

She kissed back, tasting him, laving over and under his tongue, moaning into his mouth when his touch was deep, fully embedded inside her.

Roger raised his head, breathing heavy. He husked, "Kiss me again." He lowered his head, and she did. She led the kiss, filled her mouth with his flavor, his texture, threading her fingers in his hair, slanting her head, taking what she wanted from his mouth, and ending it by sucking his bottom lip.

He blew out a long breath. "Joan, you were made for this. Your passions are as strong as mine." He raised and removed his hand, but only to brace one knee on the floor and shove up her skirts, exposing her to the waist.

"Roger!"

He took off her shoes and spread her thighs. "Scoot down, love."

"No."

He held her gaze and touched her again, explicitly, slick, and inside with a rhythm that was unmistakable.

She groaned and leaned her head back closing her eyes. She was sticky wet, feverishly hot, and there was no sense pretending that his thrusting touch was not aided by her drenched arousal. When he paused, she caught her breath, trying to remain a bit calm. But he obviously did not wish her to be.

He skimmed his palms up her thighs before saying, "Lay down for me."

"Let's wait u…"

"Why? When this feels so very good. Lay down and let me." His smile flashed in front of her half-closed eyes. "You know it does."

"But it is cramped in here." She latched onto that, half-afraid that if he did something wonderful, she was going to be groaning loud enough for the driver to hear.

"Umm. Yes." He reluctantly sat up and across from her. "No, don't cover yourself."

She did, but only to the thighs.

He winked and sighed, drawing a deep calming breath.

It was a tense ride, a hot one, and Joan was not surprised when as soon as the door of the house closed, he picked her up and carried her upstairs.

He laid her on the bed, lit a lamp, and took off his shirt in fairly short order.

"Will you remove it all?" he asked, standing by the bed, his eyes very hungry.

"Yes." She slid off, undressing and looking at him when she stood completely nude.

"Joan, you are lovely."

"Thank you." She cleared her throat, knowing she was not, but suddenly feeling it. Feeling too a new edge of excitement.

He admitted. "It is hard to resist."

She knew what he meant. "That's why this cannot go on."

Roger came behind her and walked her to the mirror. When he began to whisper, to talk to her, Joan fell into it, while he weaved that same mystical spell around and inside her. The things he said, told her and described, she now knew the feelings for, knew the image to go with them. And...he began sliding his hands around her, cupping her breasts, then laying his palm on her quivering tummy. Touching her as he murmured and whispered and talked.

With his shirt off, his masculine bronzed skin, his strength in contrast to her curves was visually arousing too, as much as the intensity on his face when Joan caught a glimpse of it.

He skimmed the curls at the apex of her thighs, lightly touching, then shaped her sides and hips with firm hands. He rubbed her buttocks and breathed hot on her neck, whispering while he filled his hands with her breasts.

Her legs were giving out, knees weak and head spinning.

Roger led her to the bed, but instead of joining her, he slid the mirror over so that she could see herself.

"Oh..." She had turned her head and realized suddenly that he'd stripped all the way down. She looked her fill while she could.

His legs were long, sturdy, buttocks taut and round. The sinew shifted when he sat behind her on the bed. Again the visual of that maleness surrounding her, watching him kiss her shoulders, nibble at her nape, and seeing raven strands of his hair brush against her own, was beyond erotic. She knew it was her with him, but it seemed dream-like, impossible that it was happening.

The room turned to another world, amber lit, sensual, an earthy scented realm, separate from all else. His heart was beating fiercely against her, and their breathing strident, lush in the chamber.

Roger was seated against the headboard, she between his legs, reclining enough to feel the scalding shape of his sex. His legs were bent, hers to the side, but she had a perfect view of them in the mirror, watching those tawny hands move over her body. He traced her throat, across her shoulders and down her arms. But when he touched her breasts and she watched him, her body did seem sexual, soft and rounded, and the nipples he'd teased to hard points seemed feminine, made for his touch.

Joan reached up, behind her, touching his face, his hair. Watching in the mirror as he turned his head, and bit lightly at her fingers, moving his lips to rub against them.

Air tight in her lungs, she whispered, "It's incredible."

He met her gaze in the reflection. Her hands covered his on her breasts, he whispered back, "Yes." Roger leaned her up, kissing down her spine, laving at the top of her buttocks before sitting her back, higher than before upon him, until his sex was between her legs.

With a soft nudge he rocked her hips, arching his.

"Oh God," she felt his silken member sliding against those nerves. "This is…"

"Yes…yes." His hands were gripping her hips, "That's it, stroke us both."

She was nearly on her knees, riding him in a way, her wet heat creating the friction for them both. Allowing him to slide easily against the receptive spot.

When he held her still, she protested with a groan. "Roger."

"Let's pace ourselves, love. We have time."

She rolled to the side and lay beside him.

Flushed and body aching, Joan had such a skin hunger that she rolled to lie atop him. Laughing breathlessly at the fact she really was much smaller than him. "I'm short." Her toes rubbed his calves.

His face showed a mixture of tense hunger and lazy arousal. "You cover enough, and feel perfect." He reached down parting her legs. She situated herself so that she sat across his upper thighs, his sex lying perfectly along her damp curls.

Joan found she liked being able to look down at him, to be this close and even, so that she could scan his face at leisure. She brushed his hair back with her fingers, letting the shoulder-length raven strands glide through them, fingering the cool silk, then tucking them behind his ears, affording a better view of his strong bones.

His hands were resting passively on her hips as she did this, his jet eyes watching her closely. She leaned down to trail her lips, slightly parted, across his forehead, and then each winged brow. His lashes were thick and blunt. She kissed his eyelids, across his high cheekbones, liking the taste of him and feeling tingles in her own body from her explorations. Still feeling heavily aroused, she glided her mouth down to his jaw, then deliberately went to that scarred side, planting soft kisses, even running her tongue down its length.

Her breath was sizzling while her body reacted to his taste and feel. She bit his chin and then found her way back up, teasingly laving toward his ear. His hands tightened when her lips were against it.

She whispered, "You feel so good, taste so good." Her lips found a spot just below his ear, to kiss then to lave and she bit at his skin. She felt him arch under her, felt his fingers flex again, hearing him murmur something deep and raw.

But she was stimulated, getting wetter, more aroused from his taste, she suckled hard, her rapid breath echoing back at her from his skin.

"Bloody hell." Roger arched his head back then, giving her all the access she wanted.

Joan wanted. She laved and bit, sucked across his strong neck, to the other side, then down his throat. The sinew was flexed tight, and the skin warm and musky with manly flavor. Sexually excited by the tension in his body, that tremble in him, she kissed his collarbone, across his broad shoulders, and bit at those corded arms. Joan slid her palms up, touching his face as she went lower across his upper chest, finding his tight, male nipple and suckling him as he had her.

"Christ..." His voice was rough, taut. His hands went to her hair, splaying on her head while she moved from one to the other.

She moaned, moving her head in circles and feeling sexual chills over her body. Feeding off his pleasure, she dragged her palms down, letting her fingertips rub those hard nubs while she slid back and finished her journey, kissing down the center of his stomach, laving and biting those ridged muscles, and lingering at his navel. Able to feel the quiver in the underlying sinew.

"Joan, Joan, Christ..." He was trying to raise her head. He sounded different than she'd ever heard him and so did she. Her eyes fogged with kindled fires and burning desire. He was delicious, warm, his taste easily addictive. And the look in his eyes stirred her feverishly hot. Lids nearly closed, those black eyes glowed febrile, nostrils flared, lips parted, his breathing harsh, he looked as out of his head as she felt.

His tongue came out to wet his lips. Roger slid his hands from her hair, firmed them on her spine, and brought her to him for a sizzling, viscous kiss that was mingled breaths, velvet tongues and wet lips sliding, clinging, moving in counterpoint.

Her palms came up to rest on his cheeks while she groaned into his mouth, whimpering when the kiss grew unrestrained, until they were sucking tongues sluggishly, and biting lips and sipping each other. It was sex, as much as it could be with mouths and tongues, and it felt and tasted and was, because they were making it, sexual. Giving in to the primal and following a need to assuage the fever in their blood.

Roger used his superior weight to roll Joan to her back. Her legs were already bent and it was natural to her, to wrap them around his hips.

Breathless, nearly sobbing, she held his head as he dipped to nip and suck at her throat, nuzzling, laving, biting softly, before coming back time and again to her mouth. Her craving completely out of control, Joan arched up when her inner muscles compressed. The tease of his manhood poised so close to her damp heat seemed to drive her wild.

Joan turned her head, to catch her breath and gasp, "Please…please, I want you…"

He had been braced on his forearms, his body touching her, yet keeping his weight lighter. Roger's groan filled her ear before he raised his head, using his hand to nudge her so that he could see her face.

Hotter than fire, burning up, she felt somewhere between tears and complete and utter desperation, her only thought was being filled by him. "It's not like before," she whispered, low. "Not just that release, but I have to have…I need…"

"I know…" he whispered, tensely. "But it would be over too soon at this point."

"Roger." She felt like weeping.

"I'll give you what you need, love. What we both need, but trust me just a bit more." He kissed her before sliding down her body, all the way, until his mouth was buried against that aching heat.

"Oh…aaaaaah." She fisted her hands in the coverlet at the first touch of his tongue. Flames licked through her with every stroke of it. When he widened his mouth and sucked hard where she ached explicitly, she was engulfed in a swift and intense climax that summoned a low-pitched sound from her throat, echoing around the room.

He slid up her again, and holding her legs open, he slid his sex over and across her wetness. She came again. His seed flowed, scalding hot on her thighs, mingling with her own climax.

~

An hour later Joan was in the bathing chamber, having made use of the scented oils, and having finished the wine that Roger had poured for her, before heading there. She had finished bathing and wrapped herself in a thick towel after drying, using the comb to brush her hair back.

She returned to the bedroom, finding the fire lit and the lamp turned up, enough to illuminate the room yet not harsh, more of mild saffron that retained the aura of intimacy.

Roger had bathed and apparently straightened the bed, and the mirror was against the wall, she noticed, so that the fireplace was reflected in it.

He sat on a blanket in front of the fire, wearing only his trousers, his raven still-wet hair slicked back and skin scented from manly soap. The bottle of wine was there, and one glass, and a platter of fruit.

Joan sat down a foot from him, warmed by the gentle heat of the fire. She crossed her legs and reached for one of the plums, rolling it in her palms before biting into it.

The haze of greed was gone, but the tension and awareness remained sharp. She allowed herself to look at him, to study his profile. His pose was one of deep thought as his legs stretched out, one palm down to bear his weight, and the other hand holding his shorter glass, which she knew was brandy, resting the bottom of it on his thigh.

His profile was both illuminated and shadowed by the movement of the fire. It turned his skin to dark satin, flattering the hollows, sinew-enhancing his maleness in a primitive way. Even the fact that his hair was wet, that she was seeing him just after a bath, gave an aura of the forbidden to his image.

She was in deep waters, she told herself.

Something in her chest constricted just looking at him, something more than that desire to have him in the ultimate, most intimate way. She told herself not to examine or think, not to spoil what time she had by sifting through every feeling. There were too many, too new, and she could feel the seconds slipping away.

She finished the plum and reclined on her side slightly opposite him, so that she was looking at his face.

Roger's eyes flickered to her. He stared for a long time, quiet, yet seeming to probe intently. "Are you ready to leave?" His tone was soft, and casual despite the thoughts masked in his eyes.

"If you still want, I'll take this night with you." She had decided that fairly early in the evening. Now she felt as if she *had* to have him, some part of him, deep inside. Another intense feeling she was not going to pick apart.

"And then, you'll quit the season, return home?"

"Yes."

He dropped his gaze to her mouth, then brought it back. "And live your life without a man?"

"That's the idea." She smiled, a little strained. "In spite of this, what we are doing. I don't see myself having numerous lovers and affairs. There's been opportunity before, and I know I don't want that. I never felt this intensity for anyone. I know that you can do this with other women, but I can't with other men." She looked away a moment. "Not even thinking myself in love years ago, felt like this." Her eyes met his. "I understand the carnal lure of sex, the lust, and I understand the hunger that brings two strangers together. But it doesn't happen like that with everyone, not for me. It never has."

"You think that every sexual encounter is moment by moment what we've done?"

She pushed up, her weight now on her elbow. "I assume it is close enough."

Roger shook his head. "There are heated encounters, fleeting and fast, and there are arrangements where release is the objective. But you wanted intimacy and, I think, that takes a relationship of sorts, more of having to trust each other. The other women were vastly more experienced. It was carnal and lust, and that was all."

"I realize you made concessions." She smiled knowing he was growing weary of telling her over and over how different this was, but, "I may as well have been a virgin, for all that I knew."

"You have only just begun."

"I know that." She bit her lip. "I should likely thank you, for being the sort of lover you are with me."

His smile echoed hers. "I gained as much, or more, than you did from it. In the norm, if you will, of my rakehell life there is nothing like this, and it is as heady being the tutor watching you react, as it was an hour past, being the focus of your desire to taste and touch me. You have a natural essence of sensuality that more practiced females cannot match, Joan. Do not thank me, because that was supremely more arousing, than anything I can recall." His smile faded and he added honestly, "You act from the core of your passions, and they are much more, than even I could have imagined."

More than I'd imagined too, Joan thought, recalling the desperate hunger and the consuming fire, the wholly untamed need for everything he'd give her—and yes—she'd wanted to do much more to him than she had. On some level, she'd let go, and on another, she'd restrained herself.

93

Roger's gaze held hers again. He asked smoothly, "If I did not have the past, the reputation that I do now, would that make any difference?"

"I suppose I'm thankful you gained your skill and finesse."

He laughed. "That's not what I mean."

"I know." She sighed. "Would I have a long term affair, sexual affair, with you—if I did not know you were sleeping with other women?"

"You give me too much credit," he said dryly. "I'm not sleeping with other women at the moment, not since meeting you."

Her brow raised.

He shrugged. "There's only so many hours in the day, love. And, I was blunt, I want you, and I do not happen to have a desire for another whilst I do."

"I'm sincere enough to be grateful then, because there's something in me that balks at imagining you kissing me or touching me, and doing the same hours later with another woman. It may be true, I assumed it was, but I couldn't think about it. I could not have kissed your body and done that. 'Tis likely a woman's peculiar way of thinking..." She shrugged and sat up, re-tucking the end of the towel that had come undone.

He had watched that motion. "I was aware of that."

She believed that he was. Joan looked around the room. "Do you do that...with other women?'

"What?"

"Use that pet name you sometimes call me by...call them, love?

"No."

She brought her eyes to his. "What do you call them?'

"Nothing. I rarely talk to them at all." He smiled and cocked a brow. "You must attend what I say. It may be difficult for someone like you to comprehend, but lust is as common as eating. Sexual encounters are for only that."

"Yes. I did forget that."

He reached out and tugged one of the curls that had dried and fallen over her forehead. "'Tis because you are not jaded, so don't assume that sort of woman or man is superior. You have far more appeal."

When he lowered his hand she nodded, secretly thrilled that he thought so. She stared at him, her thoughts open to read. "We have a few more hours..."

His eyes were motionless, quiet. "Since you intend to end the...association, after tonight...are you sure that is the way you wish to do it?"

"I thought that was your goal, your intent from the first kiss you stole," she whispered. "You wanted me...that way."

"Yes." His tone seemed distant. "I did."

"But you do not, now?"

"I want you more," he returned calmly. "But between then and now, you have become more than... an object of lust, a sexual encounter I desired." His smile was self-mocking. "In letting you set the rules, and in bringing you to this point, I've gotten to know you in a way, that makes it more complicated than a seduction."

That surprised her.

Mostly, because she had felt that way too—felt that she was closer to him in some ways than just the sexual.

She saw him turn back to stare, brooding, into the fire. He did know more about her than anyone else did. He knew this, the most exposed things. She wasn't sure she knew him really, but what she knew of him was surprising, and it was what cost her sleep. That affectionate pat he'd given the old duke, the fact that he scowled when around the ton, but smiled often around her. He was considered a rake, and a hard man, even a sinister one, but she knew a man whose voice was smooth and deep, alluring, and sometimes...almost loving. He wasn't selfish, ruthless, and demanding with her...he was sexual, sensual, and... his touch, the way he looked at her, the words he spoke when weaving that erotic spell...no, that man was unique...and he was not the man others were familiar with.

Joan thought about those last moments in bed. Her skin sensitized remembering how, when kissing his face, and laving his skin, he'd trembled. How he'd burned, given in, allowing her explorations to take him under the spell too. She knew instinctively he wasn't like that with other women...she just knew it. He was showing her things, hidden and contained things, that no one saw. He did all of that for her... It wasn't as if he simply couldn't control it, more as if he'd reached a point of knowing when he could not, and at that point, he trusted her...he surrendered in essence.

She had something of Lord Roger that no other did. She absorbed the truth of that. She had the man behind the rakehell, the real one, who, but for the incidents that forced him to take on that cloak, that shell of distance, would be entirely different. She did not know everything about the years before she met him, she knew there were closed doors and things a man like him did not share with others. But she did not believe they were weaknesses or evil that tainted him. He was too giving for that, and he touched her...kissed and stroked her, too much like a man intent on pleasing.

Other feelings attached to that realization—possibilities that made her heart race, but she was a grown woman and this time, she was the willing fool, because in her heart she knew it was worth it. This time she chose to take what she could get, and deal with consequences later.

Joan tugged the end of the towel and let it fall. She closed the distance, and on her knees at his side, she used her hands to turn his gaze toward her. He lost that far away look instantly, his hands came up to rest at her sides the same moment his gaze skimmed down the front of her before returning to meet her own.

She held that look while she lowered her head, inching closer to his mouth, and a breath away she husked, "Make love to me…"

His harsh groan was lost in the sleek kiss she gave him. That arm snaked round until he pulled her across him. Then his hands were cupping her head.

They kissed long and passionately, over and over, in every variation, and their breath turned hot, their tongues stroked, open lips rubbed each other's taste and mingled it. His head moved, slanted when he wanted depth, when he wanted to plunge and ravage and fill her mouth with his touch.

Roger pushed off his trousers and shifted, rolling her to her back, and poising himself between her legs. They had to break the kiss to fill their starved lungs with air.

Joan's hands were on his sides. She caressed him while they gazed at each other, the labored breaths wafting between wet lips. She was conscious of her nipples, tight and stimulated by his chest, her inner thighs tingling from his hard heat and masculine skin between them, the core of her, wet, ready, aching, while her eyes took in everything about his intense expression.

She felt his deep rasp rumble in his chest when he husked, "I'll protect you from pregnancy, but for a few moments, I want to feel you."

Somewhere in the haze she knew what he meant. She wet her lips, her fingers tightening on his sides. "I want this. I want to feel every second of it. It is the first real time for me, needing and craving…I want to savor every moment."

His raven lashes dipped, eyes closed a moment. "Joan." He opened them, swallowed, and licked his lips. "Raise your knees, love."

She did, higher on his hips. Arching her head back to look at him, as his greater height put him above her. Weight braced on his hands and knees, his taut features exposed to her, he watched her too.

The smooth, round tip of his sex spread that delicate entrance. He shuddered again, rasping, "Now, love?"

"Yes, please...yes." Her heart was near to bursting, her plea more a tight cry.

He flexed his hips, sinking in slowly.

Joan's lips parted wide, her moan, a loud one. Her lashes fluttered, thighs trembled with each inch of him that filled her. Her hands shifted to his arms, nails scouring, while she absorbed the delicious, incredible feel of him.

He exhaled harshly and seemed to stop completely once fully embedded, bodies locked tight, her silken heat milking, contracting, against the shape and length, and the fullness that seemed made for it.

Roger began to move, shallow, only inches out, and languidly.

She was already arching up, into it, already bowing and panting from the flames racing up her spine, the intense pleasure from his movements.

"Oh...Roger...yes...yes...oh God...it feels so good."

"Joan," he growled and slid out further, in harder.

She kept pace, chasing that feeling, reaching greedily for the sensations of his slick strokes. Her sounds filled the room. She didn't care, she whispered and she cried out, and she growled out the incredible response she was experiencing each time his flesh stroked her that way.

At some point Roger reached down and held them both still, catching his breath. Then rising up on his knees, holding her hips high and arched tight to him, while he looked at her.

Her face was flushed, and white teeth sank into her bottom lip. Her eyes glittered like sunlight through emeralds, and her petite body, creamy and curved and bathed in sexual chills, vibrated with hunger.

He shook his head from side to side, arching his neck to gasp some air, his eyes nearly rolling back he managed, "This is the best it has ever felt...Joan, you're incredibly hot and pulsing against me." He lowered his head, seeing a tear run from the corner of her eye. "I want to lose myself in you."

Her teeth released that swollen lip, her tongue soothed the spot, and he felt her shudder against him as she whispered, "You're making it so very good. I want to feel more. I want you to take me deeper."

"Christ, Joan." Sliding his hands to the underside of her thighs he held those creamy limbs wide and with her hips high, he sank hard once, to see if she could take it.

"Yes!"

Her growl was all he needed. He pulled back and slammed in hard, over and over, feeling the slick heat of her inner walls stroke and squeeze him back. And it was the best sex had ever felt for him, every inch sensitive and every sense aware of her musk scent, her whispers and moans, of her body pulling him back, greedily, and of each arch of her hips riding him hard.

He leaned forward, letting her limbs slide over his arms, curling his body into hers and filling everything she had until she whispered that she could not take another inch. When he felt his sac tightening, his inner thighs beginning to quiver, he knew he was going to explode. He knew too, it was going to be the ultimate.

Joan knew it too. She felt the subtle swell inside her and in spite of the fact he had thrust deep and out a dozen times, she was already regretting he'd pull out. But he did, and spilled his seed in the soft curls between her legs, shuddering and breathing heavily by her ear, muttering an explicit phrase that somehow did not shock her. In fact she smiled despite the dazed feeling—he'd paid her the ultimate compliment.

After she'd gotten up and refreshed herself, Joan returned from the bathing room, just as he did. Roger prevented her from sitting on the quilt and instead placed her forward in his lap, kissing her while he stroked her body close to climax.

Her hands on his upper arms, she moved with the touch, listened to his sensual words, and reached one hand down when the intensity had gathered to a tight, centered point, guiding his finger inside her, reaching her peak and falling against him.

Roger had fixed the fire. They lay under one of the light blankets, Joan on her stomach looking into the flames, and Roger on his side facing her, his hand occasionally stroking her spine, her buttocks, her hair. Joan realized that moments were fleeting, and she thought of something he'd husked when he was plunging deep in her. He'd said that it could not be the last time, that he wanted more and more.

A shuddered sigh escaped her, lashes fluttering closed. It had been incredible, beyond her imaginings. It made up for the horrid experiences she'd had when younger, and made her realize what she would have missed if she'd let those experiences keep her from ever being intimate again. It was day to night, and she realized what type of man Robert had been. Thank God she had not wed him.

She must have dozed because her body was heavy, relaxed when she felt Roger touch her again.

He rolled her more to her side and slid her leg upward, and stroked her gently, until she was wet, ready. Joan's heavy lids lifted only slightly when he entered her that way, shifting deep and filling her, until there was no room and their bodies cinched inside, sex to sex.

She sighed softly, gave a moan of sleepy pleasure, and caressed his muscled thigh.

He brought his lips to her ear, letting her hear his excited breaths when he began to move rhythmically in and out. Rocking against her, into her, Roger's masculine breathing told her he was feeling it, loving it, enjoying her.

Joan's blood heated by degrees, simmering and stirring until her heart thudded and her breaths began to match his. Her nails dug into his flank. She whispered his name pushing against his thrusts.

He whispered back, sensual, sexual things, dark and sweetly erotic, telling her how she felt to him. When he shuddered and pulled back, his cry was grit from the depth of him, that he did not want to leave her, that he wanted to be in her when he exploded.

~

It must have been the edge of dawn when Joan left him sleeping on the blankets and roused the driver herself. She dozed much of the way back to her house, and fell into bed with that same *walking in a dream* feeling. Dreaming of the hours that had passed and knowing she would never feel that again.

At noon, she sent word to Lecrox manner, and had the servants begin packing her things. She wrote a letter to Uncle Willy, and forced plenty of cheerfulness into it. Then more formal notes she penned to the hostesses who had entertained her, giving Miss Avery a list to take to the floral shop by way of thanking them.

Since her Uncle Willy owned the house, she had only to await her coachman and footmen from Lecrox, who should be arriving the following day.

Joan sent a note round to Simon, filled with the sort of advice he hated, telling him to come and see her during the off season, admonishing him to take care of himself and curtail a bit of his raking.

She sat upstairs late evening, pen in hand, and pad on her lap, whilst she looked down at the streets and wondered if she should write to Roger. Leaning her head against the raised window, she realized there was no way to convey to him what she felt about their time together. It was an affair that she had been adamantly against, but one that she would appreciate for the rest of her life. He'd shown her bliss and brought her amazing pleasure, and she felt she understood what being a woman meant so much more now. She understood her mother, and that wonderful relationship her parents had shared, that closeness and the long looks, the lingering touches they used to exchange.

101

Everything her mother had tried to tell her as a girl made more sense. She only comprehended it now because Roger was a man who was made for women. One who enjoyed the full bloom of their passions, and who had the intensity and focus, the care, to make sex an equally satisfying experience.

Thus, she sat there, unable to write a word, because words would never describe in any real way, where the journey had taken her.

Chapter 10
Lecrox Manor November, five months later

"Going out for a ride, are ye?" Joan's maid Agnes was putting away clothing in the wardrobe, and looking over her shoulder.

Agnes was in her late fifties, and had been her maid since she was a child. She, like the entire household, had met Joan's return with smiles and happy chatter, everyone over the weeks questioning her about London and the season, scolding her because she hadn't brought home a husband.

But Agnes, who'd known the less formal manner of the household, since her father's time, was quite used to Joan riding year round. They'd had three weeks of dreary rain and brooding clouds that had finished turning the fall leaves to brilliant golds and reds and, other than visiting tenants, and doing estate business, Joan had been stuck inside.

"I need to stir about." Joan smiled and buttoned the heavy, doeskin riding jacket. "We've actually got sun today. I enjoy a spring rain, but I can do without this dreary weather."

"Aye. You and me both. My joints be aching, and the whole of the house seems glum and dreary. I'll not be smiling when the snows come either. The 'ouse be too quiet these days, milady."

"I'm the Joan I was before I had a season," Joan scolded. "You've all milady'd me to death since I got back." She pulled on her gloves. "Last week I was in my trousers, mucking stalls with Hobbs, and he was milady this and milady that."

"Your parents had titles," Agnes sniffed. "Your mother expected us to use them…"

"Agnes." Joan put her hands on her hips and regarded her wryly. "You wiped my nose and my bottom, I'll do

103

with the formality in public, but you're all like my family here."

"Not if you'd get yourself a husband." Agnes grumbled and shut the wardrobe doors, turning and placing her hands on her own amble hips. "You should have a family of your own. Your mother wanted it, and your father too."

Joan laughed. "Oh yes, I should have brought all of you one of those London lords." She chuckled. "Pasty and white and carrying hankies with more lace than is on your cap." She winked. "He'd likely retire here a few weeks out of the year, but keep me—"

"They're all not that way!" Agnes cut her off grunting. "I read the Times too. You should 'av brought us one those chaps like yer father. A real man."

Should have brought them a...Joan crossed her arms, her eyes going over the woman suspiciously. "What do you know Agnes?"

"Not a thing." Agnes tried to contain her smile.

"Uh...hum." Joan tapped her boot against the hardwood floor.

Agnes bit her lip then laughed and spread her arms, "Oh all right. We heard a bit of gossip during the season, and we was hoping."

"Gossip?"

"Yes, about you and a certain earl."

Joan's eyes widened. "Rea-lly. What exactly did you hear?"

"Not much. Just at the start of the season there was some. Well Lady Viv's maid said, that the Duke's footman told her, that Lord Wythe's driver heard it from his valet—"

"Heard what?"

"That he was pursuing you."

"The man has a reputation."

"Oh, pish, I know that. So did yer da. One of the biggest, blackest rakehells in London yer mum said."

Joan sighed. "Well. It was all rumors. Lord Wythe and I attended many of the same parties, and we liked each other well enough. But I did not go to London to catch a husband."

"More's the pity." Agnes sighed and headed for the door. She threw over her shoulder before going out in the hall, "But Charles the gardener, heard from the butcher, that Lord Wythe returned two months ago. He spent a month aboard his ship, and then, 'tis rumored that he's set to getting Black Cross in order."

"Bloody hell." Joan muttered when the door closed with a click. Likely the entire staff knew more than they were letting on and just as likely, they had been talking about it the whole bloody time she'd been home.

A half-hour later Joan was on her muscled gelding, galloping along the back road toward Black Cross. She'd planned on going there before Agnes spoke, purely out of curiosity of course. She had no intention of riding up to the front door, but she'd thought of Roger daily, nightly, and while she'd got on with life, even enjoyed it, she was human enough to spend some restless hours lost in those memories. Weak enough to ramble through the gardens and meadows, trying to work through the ache that the memories awakened anew.

It wasn't as chilly as it had been early that morning, and though her doe jacket was light, it provided enough covering with her tan riding skirt and cream blouse. She'd had her hair cut as soon she'd returned home, wearing a scarf to market on some days, bonnets and hats in public, but noticing that fashion was changing to allow shorter locks and more simplistic styles. She could only be grateful, because compared to the season and London, she preferred her country life with its freedoms. She didn't want to be stuck with unmanageable hair simply because fashion dictated it.

She'd ridden over an hour, before the soaring spire of Black Cross could be seen against the lighter sky. Joan slowed the mount and eyed that Latin symbol, knowing that the stones of the main structure, and the walls, were actually a darkest gray that appeared black when wet. She wasted a few moments recalling having made the ride with both her parents, sighing at the best memories and realizing she was never going to stop missing them.

Joan kneed the horse into a steady but fast pace, not slowing until she cut off the main path, and under the iron arches, eyeing the winged walls of the original fortress, seeing the distant orchard, as well as a pair of shaggy dogs romping along the tree line. There were some very young sheep bleating in the far pasture, and she spied a few horses running along the rise of the still green hills.

She slowed the animal on the curving path leading to the front of the building—a covered courtyard that led to massive arched doors. On the sides and around the old church, were some of the most beautifully laid gardens and old gothic statuary. She had no idea how many acres the main grounds included, but there was a lake beyond the trees, which was a haven for ducks and geese and other wildlife. She recalled from childhood that there were several other buildings scattered about, but they had been barred and locked and the windows iron-shuttered. All of which had added to her dramatic fancy about the place when she was growing up.

Joan halted just inside the courtyard, leaning down to pat the horse's steaming neck while looking at the façade. Above her, the main building soared and spread out. She reckoned it had at least three stories, and an attic-like top story before the open belfry.

A dull thudding sound drew her gaze to the right. She turned the mount, curious enough to follow the flagstone route to discover the source. She rounded the corner and scanned the long passage, open in places with arched entries and running the length of the building. Likely the rear access way, since the old framework used to have separate entrances and exits.

She kneed the mount to a sedate walk, and spied the oiled wood doors beyond the shadows.

About center-way she saw him, hammering one of the iron pins into the door that had likely loosened with age.

He wore a collarless white shirt, billowing and damp with sweat between his shoulder blades. His raven hair was longer than in London, and he wore buff trousers, much like the locals, and calf-high boots of supple brown leather.

Joan grinned dryly, measuring his height and breath against that solid door, and the rough-hewn stones, thinking that she'd been right about the perfect setting, for he seemed quite naturally suited to the massiveness of the old place.

She winced when her horse whinnied and snorted, pawing the stones, clearly thirsty from the long ride. The old troughs were still there. She led him over, her eyes on Roger when he'd stopped hammering and turned in surprise.

"Good afternoon, my lord." She stupidly did not know what to say.

He smiled and tossed the hammer into a wooden box, wiping his hands on his trousers and striding toward the nearest arched opening, right near the trough.

"Joan." He looked her over.

She did some looking too, and though her imaginings were fairly good, she was struck anew at his swarthy skin and pitch eyes, those winged brows.

It was nothing compared to the sinew she spied when the breeze tugged that shirt, undone a few buttons, and displayed places she recalled kissing.

"I didn't expect you."

"I'm sorry. I was just out for a ride a—"

"No. No I meant to send you a note, I promised you a tour. But I thought to get the place in a bit more order." He reached out and patted the horse's face when it raised from drinking in the trough and sighed.

107

Joan held his gaze, her insides trembling with both awareness and a hope that he was not disappointed to see her.

He inquired softly, "Can you stay awhile. I'm in my dirt, but…"

"I don't want to intrude, or take you from your work."

"There's always work here." He shrugged, taking hold of the bridle. "Do step down awhile. I'll call for Rory to see to your horse."

She nodded and dismounted lightly, laughing, when he *called for Rory* by whistling sharply and then bellowing the man's name.

A lanky fellow came from around the back. He had the look of a local, wearing a tweed cap and homespun, knee high boots and possessing a leathery face. He bowed to Joan, who reached over and shook his hand instead.

The man blushed and eyed Roger who merely laughed.

"The stables are back there, still connected to the main building," he told her and handed the mount off to the groom—after giving him instructions to brush it down and provide oats.

Joan walked beside him past several doors and then waited for him to lift the heavy bolt and stepped through.

He shut it, and took her elbow lightly. "We'll enter what is becoming the kitchens. It was massive before, but I'm attempting some modernization for practical reasons." He had to duck under a beam that she walked easily under, and then released her while he walked to a pump with an iron basin, and pumped water in which he washed his face and hands.

Joan glanced around, seeing several very long wooden tables with hewn benches, a couple of wrought iron chandeliers hanging from the steep-pitched ceiling. Enormous chains were attached and threaded through hooks on the wall to lower or raise them. Each had fat, tallow candles in the holders. The hearth was big enough to stand in, and there were doors leading off to cellars and pantries and other areas.

He was drying his face when she gazed back at him again, then finger combing his hair back behind his ear. S*he knew* he'd been looking at her. The hum of chemistry that she'd worried was only still lingering in her own body, was very much present and very evident while their gazes held a moment. Somewhere above wings fluttered and a clock ticked in the distance, water trickled from the pump spout. But heat pervaded the space around them.

"How are you, Joan?" His voice seemed deep, husky.

"Well," she managed, her eyes unable to look away from the darkness of his.

He stood for several silent moments, then, after his gaze went over her again, he held out at a hand, inviting her to follow him.

The first area they stepped into, after the hall, was the main chamber. High vaulted ceilings and stained glass. Arched windows. But what struck Joan with amazement, was the contents of the room.

"It's not completely organized," she heard Roger say beside her.

Her eyes did not know where to go first amid the fascinating collection. One section of wall on the left held masks, wooden and weaved, of every size and shape. Some fierce and some with exotic feathers or animal horns, others comical, but all wondrous. And with them were weapons: blowguns, spears, crude axes, and some she was not sure how they'd be used. Aside that, were shields of all manner, some so ancient that the dye artwork was faded. Many of the smaller shields were animal skin, and marked with tribal symbols.

"They're from several islands," he told her.

"How fascinating." She glanced at him smiling and shaking her head, before looking to the right, at an entire wall of mirrors—roped, iron framed, gilt, mixed with ancient-looking ones of all sizes and eras. There was a fan-shaped one in the center that was intricately worked with silver.

On the other walls there was artwork, and she pointed out three paintings in particular that looked more modern than the obviously-famous works.

"My other estates."

They were stately. Perfect English manor houses, beautifully kept and orderly—and the opposite of the ancient church. Whoever had painted them had an eye for detail, and they very much befitted an earl.

When Joan looked back into the center of the room, she saw Egyptian sofas arranged around each of the large hearths and sectioned off by Chinese screens. There were vases taller than she was and a whole host of scrolled and embossed wooden furniture.

Her eye was drawn to a large throne chair grouped with a massive chaise with gold feet and fringe. The upholstery on the seating and hassocks was lush, rich, deep reds, jade greens, royal purples and blue velvets. Casually tossed over a large folded screen were gossamer panels of gold and silver material, artlessly mingled with patterned silks.

"No, this would not fit your other estates, but they are perfect here." She walked toward the former altar area, stopping now and again to run her hand over some wonderfully carved artifact or to lift a piece of strangely beautiful artwork from an ivory pedestal

Tall, multi-height iron candle-stands were lined up on either side of the dais of the old altar and, in the center and up three stairs, was the largest, most massive bed she'd ever seen.

"It belonged to a sultan."

She looked at Roger, laughing. "I can believe that. It's certainly large enough for an entire harem!"

"Yes." He walked toward it, and Joan stood looking up as he went to the thick, high headboard. "We had to dismantle it to get it in here, it was so heavy."

"What are all those tasseled keys?"

"Secret drawers."

"Really?"

His brow arched, his smile wicked. "They are."

"Is there anything in there?"

"Yes. Everything you can imagine and more. Would you care to look?"

"No." She chuckled. "Not at the moment."

"Too bad." He walked down toward her. "There is a mirrored canopy that hangs over it. You really should try it out."

Joan was beginning to flush. She knew he was remembering another bed at another time. "Perhaps later."

He chuckled, obviously amused, but led her through an arch, and up to the second story.

"Toys!" she stood in the doorway, looking at the crowded shelves.

"Not all. On this side, further back, are clocks and an odd assortment of things."

Joan spent a half-hour enthralled by Roger's eclectic collection. There was actually an arched bridge in the center of the room that Roger told her they'd had to take apart and put back together. It was carved with birds and forest animals. On some sections of the walls there were paintings and charcoal drawings of children from all over the world, done on everything from canvas to animal skin and parchment.

"This room surprises me," she admitted, fingering a clock with gold doors and tiny figures that turned with the seconds. She couldn't refrain from contemplating the innocence and purity of childhood as she glanced around. Such a carefree state of being, and she thought she understood why Roger collected so many things that reflected it.

"Does it?"

"Yes, I expected a rake to have totally decadent taste, like the bed below for instance, but this…"

"I did not collect things from taste. I merely picked up, in my travels, what fascinated me or in some cases, something that reflected local culture." He invited her to the next level.

There Joan observed by the light flooding through the arched windows, many things that echoed and complimented the lower floor. More amazing objects lined on pedestals, colorful stones, coral and glowing rocks, which he explained, came from mines, caves, lava, and the sea. Amid this collection were lanterns of all shapes, and books, towering shelves of books, and what she discovered were ship's logs. There were nautical instruments, antiquated maps framed on the walls, and encased in glass.

Wonderful leather sofas provided seating, yet the overriding theme on tables and wardrobes, was ships, and travel. In protective cases there were hats, helms, rings and stones that glowed with strange inner lights.

"It's like being in a museum."

"I donated quite a bit to London." He came over and showed her some of the intricately bound books.

"Were you injured during the war?" She glanced at him.

"No." He reached for a wicked looking curved sword, a cutlass that was hanging near the logbooks. "This." He turned it around then traced the scar down his face. "A pirate was aiming to lop of my head, and I managed to save it, but got quite a blow."

"He's dead I hope."

Roger laughed at her indignant tone and nodded before hanging the sword back up. "Yes. He fell over a coiled rope and hit the rail and broke his neck."

"Good," she muttered.

He said, "We'll save the belfry and lower chambers for another time. Will you join me for lunch?"

"I didn't see any servants."

"There are a dozen or so." He led the way out. "Locals I hired. Cook is out, but I can manage something."

Below in the kitchens, she watched him roll up his sleeves and begin preparing a meal.

"You can cook?"

"Yes." He grinned, looking up from his task. "Can you?"

"Some." She took off her jacket.

They managed between them, but mostly with Roger's proficiency, to prepare a decent meal. He took it out the side door, bringing wine and sliced bread. They sat where the weak sun was arcing in, and ate.

Joan asked about the building and lands, listening to the sound of his deep, resonant voice, not at all surprised that he had researched it thoroughly. By the time the meal was done, they sat holding their glasses, feet propped on a low bench, easily discussing the port city and exchanging information on the economy.

Roger looked at her saying, rather like a revelation had just struck his brain, "You actually do run your estates."

"Yes."

"It must have been quite stifling during the season, playing the typical role that females seem to be placed in."

"I did it for Uncle Willy. And for my mother. My father too, honestly. Though he taught me to run my inheritance, he allowed my mother to balance out my training with all the normal female instructions." She smiled wryly. "I imagine it kept me out of trouble, most of the time, because of my independent streak."

He got up and stepped inside and came back smoking a cheroot, this time leaning against the arch, almost in front of her, studying her as he smoked.

"It's very difficult here, now, imagining you losing your head, or your heart."

She nodded. "I expect it was stubbornness, and perhaps something I had to go through. I suppose, I had to learn it the hard way, because I still had so many girlish dreams to get past, before growing up. I saw some of that amid the debs of the ton. I should have envied it, but I

113

would find myself thinking that down the road, they will be in for a rude awakening."

"But your parents had a good marriage?"

"Yes. Based firmly in reality." She chuckled. "They loved and argued, and played and were partners. They were strong-willed people who made perfect sense. Although in some ways, they were opposites."

She watched the breeze tug his hair and asked, "Did your parents have a good marriage?"

"Typical." He shrugged. "He was lord, master, tyrant, and she was submissive. I don't recall that she did much but entertain and shop. When she spoke it was normally not an opinion, but rather father's dictates."

"That's the way of it."

"Yes," he agreed sardonically. "I imagine that he decided to turn his back on me and she went along with it, without a protest."

"Perhaps if they'd lived longer, it would have worked itself out."

"My father," Roger said, "was a man of uncompromising will. Everything was black or white to him. He was wealthy enough, influential enough, to cut whom he chose. I do not expect that his arrogance would have allowed him to amend his decision." He added, "All that I recall of him is connected to those times when he felt I needed to be reminded of what he expected of me and that, more often than not, included a list of standards that he deduced I was nowhere near reaching. In his view, I was not going to measure up anyway. Who could, to his lofty heights?"

"That's a pity. You're an extraordinary man. And in spite of being a, well a rogue, and earning it, there's much more to you than that. Your parents missed knowing an interesting man. Most of society has."

His gaze was quiet on hers. "And you, are much more than you let on in London."

She smiled slightly. "I'm sure amid the ton, there are a vast number of people who have lives outside that role." She stood and looked out at the sky. "I must be heading back."

"Allow me to send for the coach?"

"No. Thank you, it is clear enough yet. I expect the rain is done for a few days."

~

Later Roger gave her a leg up. When the groom left, he rested his hand on Joan's boot. "Are you coming back again?"

She gathered her reins and gazed down at him. "If you'll let me know when you're not busy, I'll visit at a better t—"

He cut her off, "Joan, come back whenever you like."

She sensed something in that quiet invitation and nodded, heading out then, knowing he stood there until she was out of sight.

Roger watched her disappear and swallowed the tense knot in his throat. He released a breath that seemed trapped in his lungs the whole of the time she was there. Pushing the loose strands of his hair back out of his face, he turned to finish working on the door. She would be coming back.

Chapter 11

She did go back, three days in a row, and then twice the next week. Joan finished the tour, though she could never tire of exploring the place, and was between horror and laughter realizing there were crypts and coffins in the dungeon of the building. She snorted when Roger shrugged, saying that the dead did not bother him, and that whatever spirits might roam the structure and grounds, they were peaceful ones, who seemed content with him being there.

On one of their excursions, they were deep in the bowels of the old tunnel and though it was early morning, Joan felt the sense of darkness and stillness, the absence of time disturbing this hidden part of the old church.

Roger held the lantern aloft and reached for her hand. They looked down into the murky cistern that was fed from an underground water source.

Having made her way through cobwebs and breathed in the dank smell of mold, Joan was conscious of the water trickling off the stones, and the hidden depth of the well. Conscious of a sense of suspended and shrouded time that had stopped when the old church had ceased to be in use.

Voices quiet, yet echoing in the narrow passage, she asked, "Can I touch it?"

He nodded and set the lantern down. Keeping a secure hold on her hand while she reached out and dipped her fingers in it.

"It's so cold."

"Yes. "

She stood and watched the rippled patterns fade out to nothing, speculating on what might have taken place in the tunnels, and Joan of course, wondered if murder and mayhem had happened in that very pool.

Roger laughed. "I would not doubt it. Every old place has its darker side."

"As every person does." She nodded. "But perhaps there were lovers' trysts or this was a refuge, a hiding place in more turbulent times? I'd rather think that." She smiled. "Maybe this secret place succored some soul who was in need of a hiding place because of someone evil."

Roger murmured, "Some say that every building has a presence, and I've been in less aged ones that felt darker and colder, less welcoming. Whatever they are here, they aren't sinister and evil. I've felt that sense of being watched, some force around me at times. It doesn't feel threatening."

"Perchance, they're pleased because you didn't let the thing fall to ruin, and they're around because you're making repairs, bringing real life back here. I must admit, it felt good to ride up and see servants about and flocks in the fields. You're breathing life back into something that others cast off."

"Perhaps."

Joan thought as they moved on, *just as you did to me when I was convinced that there was nothing more, and that my future path would be a solitary one.*

She may not have been cast off or forgotten like the old church, but her family, save Uncle Willy, the people who'd made her feel protected and secure, who had fostered her dreams, they were no longer. She knew that when the shock of her parent's death had worn off, she'd closed up places and sealed off rooms that might have remained opened if they were there to care, and know, and help her plan. Sometimes the joys she'd anticipated weren't as magnificent as she'd thought, simply because she had few people to be pleased for her, or to share them with, or to know what mattered.

She shook off her thoughts, mocking herself for falling back into ones that crept upon her out of nowhere. Laughter—that was one of the things she recalled about her father. She wanted to carry the good pieces of them into her twilight years. That ability to feel free and to laugh, and maybe someday, to feel the sense that she'd made them proud. Honored their love and their memory by living her life feeling the real things and deep down, faced even the concealed things, mistakes, the unknown, decisions and choices, without fear.

They explored two more tunnels, one of which came out near the main gate. They retraced their steps and then took an off-shoot, and went upstairs, finding themselves in the old cellar.

"Wine casks?"

"Yes. And moldy cheese." He pointed to a web-covered shelf.

"Well at least the mice were well fed over the years."

They were wandering around at will, exploring whatever they could see. He set the lantern on the exit stairs. Joan slid what she thought was a dusty box off a high shelf. She dusted it with her fingers, seeing a slight pattern and blinked. "I think, this is silver."

Roger came over standing slightly behind her. "Open it," he encouraged.

She held it aloft and searched for a latch, finding it just under the lip, and lowering it to open the box. The lining was royal purple velvet and nestled within it was a gleaming, silver cup. Half-spilling from the rim was a crucifix on a beautiful chain. "Likely a communion cup?" she breathed, amazed at the shimmer and the perfect condition.

"Yes."

She traced each piece and looked at it, before turning to glance up at Roger. Her forehead brushed his chin before she pulled back with a murmur of apology.

He was in the process of picking up the cup from its bed, but stopped then because she was still looking. His eyes went to hers.

Joan wet her lips, feeling her body tingle. "It's likely very old. Medieval perhaps?"

He did not look away from her. "Possibly."

"You should probably take it above and clean it up."

"Yes." His head was descending by inches toward hers.

"There are probably dozens of things buried down here that m—"

His mouth landed on target.

Joan moaned softly, wishing her hands were not occupied with the box.

Roger was kissing her, taking the box out of her hands, and blindly setting it on the nearest shelf. Next, he turned her with a hand on her shoulder, lifting her off the ground when the embrace became full, crushing her mouth with a kiss that was so hungry she reached up, buried her fingers in his hair, and surrendered.

They were breathing harshly, the sound echoing in the dark space when he lifted his head, at the same time slowly lowering her to her feet.

Joan was unsteady when he let her go, and collected the box. She stayed that way, as if he'd stirred embers into a flickering flame, until she rode home some hours later.

~

On the third week since her visit, Joan had her trousers and a simple blouse on under a long cloak, dressing the way she was apt to at her own home, the way her mother had many times on their jaunts. She handed the horse over to Rory, answering his polite, if bashful, greeting with a smile and thanks for his care of her mount last time. She was noticing more servants this visit, a gardener wearing a wide hat and pushing a wheeled cart, and two maids who were in the kitchens, busy from the looks of things and concocting something that smelled heavenly.

"He's in the main room milady." One of the maids told her when she inquired after their master. "We've laid lunch in there at his request."

"Thank you." Joan nodded and asked their names, discovering one was a distant kinswoman of her parlor maid. She did not remove her cloak until she entered the main area, smelling and feeling the crackling fire, sighing at the bright golden glow and welcoming woodsy scent. She spied Roger sitting in one of the large chairs flanking the fireplace. The winged-back piece suited him, obviously comfortable for his height and build, something she had noted that was missing in a London parlor, where delicate pieces and stiff seating seemed preferred.

A low table of some reddish wood held several covered trays and silverware, two beautiful old plates, beside each was a wine goblet awaiting the contents of the decanter to the side.

He stood as she neared. Joan took in all black clothing, the shirt some silken material, embroidered and having a banded collar. His hair was tied back loosely, a shorter strand worked lose near his temple. In essence, he was his usual, handsome self. She did not know why other women, insipid ones, thought his scar repulsive or that it somehow marred him. She knew many women did, but it suited him perfectly as far as she was concerned. Not to mention, it must have been bloody painful and quite devastating to receive.

"The weather is turning cooler. Not cold yet, but I can smell winter creeping up." She pushed back her wool hood and pulled off her gloves.

"Yes. I had the fire laid and we're attempting to finish the out of door projects."

His eyes were going down her, over her, and seemed to freeze when she pulled off the cloak and laid it on a chair.

Joan caught that look, laughing at the stillness in him. "What?"

He raised his gaze to hers, before moving it over the snug trousers and linen blouse again. "Do you wear that often?"

"Yes. At home. As did my mother. Under a cloak of course." She sat down.

He did too but kept looking at her.

"My staff is quite used to seeing me in them, as are most of the locals. There are women who work on the fishing boats and such, who dress like their husbands and sons. Even if they put a skirt over them. It's only in London they think it more shocking to wear trousers than cut a gown to one's, well, *that*. Or dampen their petticoats. It is perfectly ridiculous to call a dampened and all but sheer gown high fashion, and consider two garments that cover from toe to neck scandalous."

Roger murmured, "I doubt that the local garb of jumpers and wool knee trousers on some fisherman's wife elicit the same, reaction, as you would. I've no objection however." His gaze went over her again. "Feel free to wear them in my presence as often as you like."

"Are you feeding me or not?" she chuckled shaking her head at his lazy smile.

"I am." He leaned up and removed the covers, telling her to help herself. He filled his own plate, propped his boot on the low stool and pushed food around, but kept gazing at her often.

Joan reminded herself while under that gaze, that she was making an effort to know Roger, trying to be herself, where she had not been, aside from those trysts in London. It was difficult, damnably so, when the heat entered his eyes like that, and her body instantly responded. She knew what that meant, what it was now. Oh yes, he may as well have had his hands on her body.

She did not eat much, and apologized to the servants when they cleared the table, it was apparent they had taken special care. But her tummy muscles were tense, and she sat there, sipping a strong coffee and cream, which he'd recommended, looking into the fire, but knowing he rarely looked anywhere but at her.

"What would you like to see today?" he asked in a tone that showed his thoughts were more intimate, the timbre much too husky to feign otherwise.

The fire was suddenly too warm, and she suggested almost absently, "Let's climb up to the belfry," and glanced at him.

Roger's brow rose and a smile curved his lips. He looked as if he'd say something, but shrugged and nodded, reaching for her hand.

She could well imagine what he wanted to say by the way he threaded their fingers together and walked close to her. That sensual, sexual tension radiated out from him like some animal instinct. One that most likely read a few signals she'd been helpless to hide from the first day there.

Bloody hell. She rolled her eyes mentally. It actually did not lessen with time and distance, but rather lay dormant until they were around each other again.

They took the dark, narrow stairs and progressed up through the overhead door. Eventually, they stood in the bell tower, looking down and outward, scanning over the vista.

The breeze was up. An approaching rain scented the air.

Joan felt a heady sense of lightness standing in the topmost of the ancient edifice. A tangible kind of floating though she was standing on a solid surface. Everything felt and smelled different, and the scene before somehow more vast and vivid.

Roger was beside her, just behind her shoulder, gazing over her at the darkening sky and gathering clouds. They moved swiftly as if propelled by the breeze, the gust freshly stroking her face and ruffling her hair, Joan tuned to peek up at him, staring awhile, quite fascinated, at that same breeze whipping his mane, until it was unbound and fluttering against the shoulders of his black shirt. She imagined he looked similar at the helm of his ship or standing on deck. Somehow it suited him, as it would not have the dandies and fops and perfumed gents of the ton. He was made for the elements, fashioned from them in a mystic way. Midnight in his eyes and hair, warm sun in his touch, earth and fire and wind.

His gaze shifted downward and locked with her own, looking so deep that she could see her reflection, feel herself drowning, lured in a sensual way.

"You enjoy being up here, this high?"

"Yes." She was aware that the fresh air had flushed her face, that her hair was likely ruffled into the wind-blown disorder it was apt to become on outings.

"There's something exhilarating about heights, being up where the birds soar. It's frightening but there's just something unconfined I suppose."

His gaze flickered to her mouth then back up. "I'll have to take you out on to sea with me."

"I'd love that." She glanced at his mouth too and then back up. "I've sailed, but not far, and never on a large ship." Her heart was beating fast, tension fanned high and her breath scuttled out, unsteady.

She could have counted the seconds before...

"Joan," he uttered in a strained, tight whisper, then grabbed her by the shoulders, pulled her to him, and began kissing her fiercely.

Joan could only clutch his shoulders and whimper her surrender. She more than welcomed it—she hungrily filled her mouth with his flavor.

She took as much as he did and her tongue was as wildly seeking, greedy. Roger lifted her up, pressing her back, against the stone barrier, then he was moving his mouth to nip at her throat and breasts beneath her shirt.

Breathless, aroused, aflame, Joan clung to him, skin burning hot and body too famished for him, feeling the first cool drops of rain on her back, yet feeling him arching his hips into hers, and sensing the controlled hunger in him.

After he'd kissed her mouth again, he put his lips to her ear and husked, "Here, now, just once, Joan."

123

Helpless to her own hunger she rasped, "Yes...yes," and was trembling when he lowered her, shaking when he unbuttoned her blouse, and then his own shirt was open.

In between hot kisses, too-short delves of tongues and getting their shirts open, Joan touched him wherever she could get her eager hands on that warm, male skin.

Roger groaned and laved and suckled her aching breasts like a man ravenous for them.

Thunder boomed, lightening sizzled, arcing down through the charcoal sky. His hands skimmed off her trousers, exposing her to the knees. He kissed her hard, let her glimpse the echoed storm in his dark eyes, before he turned her to face the low wall, which was rib high. One hand braced on the wall, Roger slid the other down her stomach, further to massage between her curls, to pleasure her to an aching dampness while her sobbing breaths encouraged his touch.

Hands on the rough stone, head back, Joan sobbed to the point of painful hunger, "Now, please. Now."

He removed his hand and surged inside her from behind, lifting her hips with his hands and whispering something explicit and feral.

Joan cried out, a sound that was drowned by the gusting wind and thickening deluge of rain.

It was a fierce joining, rough and swift, and a burning-hot union, of flesh with flesh. He drove into her, talking, muttering, growling deeply, things that she could not hear but only feel as he drove in fast and solid.

Joan was lost to the world, lost to anything but him. With every dazzling flash of lightening her blood raced. Every rumble in the clouds reverberated through her body. Likewise when he would have drawn out to spill himself, she held him tightly bound to her, inside her, reaching back and closing her eyes, shuddering with pleasure when his hot seed pumped through his shaft and bathed her deep inside, with hot, soothing, fulfillment.

~

Arms trembling in the aftermath, sliding from the stones that had held her through her inner storm, she made discreet use of the handkerchief he produced, still trembling too hard to think of what she had done, and adjusted her clothing.

"You're wet and chilled," Roger murmured when she was standing there, arms around herself and eyes aching, watching the full storm.

Joan *was* actually fighting tears, not knowing why, but not wanting him to see them. She drew a deep, cool breath into her lungs and turned around. "I think I shall make use of your offer today and need a coach ride home."

He too was now fully dressed and was looking at her in a searching way.

She did not trust herself, the emotions had gone from excitement to pleasure, to deep and intense longing, and for some reason she suddenly felt brittle, aware that she was going to start sobbing any second, and utterly surprised, inwardly appalled by it. She must leave. *Now.*

"I'll have it prepared for you." Roger followed her to the door. "Joan?"

She could not turn around. "Thank you," her voice scraped raw from her throat.

Roger said nothing else while they descended, but apparently sensed a different, more cryptic tension in her. Having donned his cape and closing the coach door later, after she was seated inside, Roger searched her face. His voice seemingly far away in her present state. "Will you come back?"

She was staring straight ahead. Her throat tight and aching. "I think not."

"Then I shall come to Lecrox manor."

Joan looked at him then. Telling her mind to grasp, her eyes to focus.

His visage unreadable, he said, "Expect me within the week."

Joan attempted to gather her wits, but had not succeeded when he stepped back and signaled the driver. She turned eventually, facing the other seat and blinking twice. Then as if lightning indeed seared through her mind, she was pressing her unsteady hand over her eyes, clamping her teeth together tightly. But the words shook lose and would not be denied.

My God...I am in love with him.

Joan groaned and sank down in the seat. "You bloody fool," she whispered trembling. "You bloody, bloody fool." Her free fist hit the seat and ground into the leather. "This cannot happen."

But later, at home, bathed, fed only because the servants swarmed her damp frame, scolding and fretting until she was warm and dry and had eaten at least a bit of fish and bread, she sat by the large window in her chambers, wearing a robe and watching the tail-end of the storm.

Joan felt her tears sliding free, mimicking the beads of water racing down the glass panes. Her stomach hurt as if punched, but she had no choice but to simply let go, in order to draw a breath that didn't feel like a tight band. She allowed the truth to echo in her head and let the emotions flood out.

Drawing up her knees, resting her head against the casement, she wept painfully. Not a girl's tears, but a woman's astute admission that her heart was lost, completely captured, and no longer her own to give at will. It had unlocked on its own, and it had allowed those fleshly feelings to transition into something profoundly more serious. Joan covered her mouth and felt her body wrench with the sobs. It was, for a moment so overwhelming that she felt as if she had no control.

Those dreams of him in London, so vividly tasting, smelling, hearing him in her sleep. The constant thoughts of him since returning. Wondering, picturing, imagining. And the longing...yes the longing...to know him fully, to see him, hear him, to feel his passions. It all led up to this moment, a moment she'd felt when that hunger to be joined had overwhelmed them both. There was no other man on earth who could make her feel that. He was all that she wanted, thought of, dreamed of, and more.

The hour melted away in teardrops easing from sobs to a steadier gathering of her emotions.

Joan felt emptied, a bit hollow afterwards. She shuddered, sighed from her bones and soul and arose to wash her face. Holding a cloth against her tear-stained skin for some time, she then lit a lamp by her bed, and sat down in the amber glow, to stare at the polished wood floors.

The tears had cleared her mind and helped her to accept that as an adult, she needed to deal with this. It had never been part of the arrangement, not reckoned into the affair, nor welcome. Roger owed her nothing. She'd given to him freely and he had likewise to her.

She lay back on the bed, the damp cloth over her eyes and her hands on her stomach. He would be coming here, to Lecrox? Why? What had he meant by that? *The affair, of course.* She answered herself. He meant to pick it up. Her participation, no her absolute abandonment today must have been an obvious sign that she would welcome it.

Give over, Joan, do not spare yourself—you haven't been subtle about wanting to see him either, have you?

No, you deluded wretch, you simply refused to see the obvious—why?

Would she pick up the affair? Of course. She would lay with him in a heartbeat. No sense lying on that score either. But could she do that, and keep her true feelings hidden? *Well, there you go, Joan, another complication to your present revelation.*

The realization that she loved a rake suddenly made her laugh, pitifully, sounding more between a groan and a moan of utter disgust.

Joan flipped the cloth from her eyes, and snorted pathetically at herself. She positively made some unfertile choices when it came to love. If you were going to plant grain, you at least looked for fertile ground and, the groan that followed mocked her, that she was lying here mentally muttering analogies of wheat and dirt whilst she'd had the utter madness to choose Lord Wythe, the biggest rakehell, the most enigmatic man in London.

And complex, Joan. Don't forget that. So many layers, so much more to him than he showed others. The things he'd collected, most telling if she was honest, and the way he did for himself. Indeed a capable and physical man. One who took charge and ran his own life, and…and then, there was the man who made love to her. A contrast to be sure.

Joan's smile faded. She sighed so deeply it filled the shadowed room. *He'd wanted her to touch him.* That thought, that truth, just floated of its own purposefulness, like a mist through her mind.

In that room he'd wanted it, and she'd already conjectured it was an indulgence he never vocalized or expressed with other women. He did allude that intimacy was something that was theirs alone.

She deduced that maybe, only Simon, was privy to the real story behind his parents' actions, doubtless knew more than she about his early years and the dynamics in the earl's household…

Maria? He hadn't thought twice about telling her that truth however. Joan thanked the bloody idiot. Really, she thought, *thank you for being too obtuse and selfish and whatever else it was that denied you Roger. I've certainly benefited rather gloriously from it, and I assume you must be blind, cold-natured, as well as greedy, and, well, out and out imbecilic. But thanks.*

The late hour arrived when Joan felt exhausted enough to sleep, she did so with a last mental reminder, more like a chant marching past her closed lids—that she must try doubly hard to appear unchanged. That she *must* act and be the independent woman she was around Roger, and *not* appear as if to have him love her back, would be worth anything in the world...

*Which it would be...oh yes...*it would hurt a bit less in private if she thought there was one slim chance of it happening. That a man like that could feel that deep kind of love, for a woman like herself...

Chapter 12

The weak sun struggled through clouds. Roger rubbed the stallion's neck while the beast blew vaporous breaths from their energetic gallop. The day held a bit of a chill. He'd worn a cape over his thick wool sweater. Donned the usual riding trousers and black boots—ones lacking the high shine of his Hessians as they were apt to be gouged and scuffed on his recent ramblings. This particular pair he'd bought in Spain and found none to equal their supple comfort.

He did not mind the chill, and was used to colder weather. He had never grown used to hats, though he wore them during the season when the occasion dictated. The stiffer styles were one of those fashion inventions that he'd dreaded from the time he was a lad. He laughed mentally, thinking that Joan's observations were starting to crop up more often in his own thoughts. They had similar dislikes for anything that confined them.

It occurred to him, as he sat there looking at Lecrox manor, taking it in, that he had likely been more himself around Joan than any other person outside of Simon or Captain O'Brian and the crew of *The Nighthawk*. In his more private moments, when he could not censor his musings, he was aware that Joan Lecrox knew more of that personal side of him than anyone did.

Roger was no longer certain, or clear, of the exact moment he'd let his guard down, though he was aware he had, with a kind of fascinated disquiet that hung constant in his thoughts. He would sometimes pause in mid motion and think, *what is it about her that makes that possible? I have had bodies, had sexual affairs, had other women.*

But no clear answer came either, because he'd not spent the time, the hours with others in order to find out. Nor had he ever developed a relationship, and intimacy—that brilliantly mysterious word he'd tossed out to lure her in—had sometimes had him struggling for control when he was never supposed to not be in control.

His gaze had begun taking measure of Lecrox from the moment he'd passed the markers. Roger was impressed, somehow not surprised that the subdued wealth of the place stood in contrast to the more ostentatious estates. He saw carefully cultivated lands, well-maintained dwellings, sleek, prime livestock.

The main buildings were impressive, suited to the climate and surroundings, the stables extensive. He eyed a carriage house, that was well able to hold several apartments for grooms and coachmen, as well as viewing some structures scattered in the now-dormant flower gardens and hedge rows, that likely afforded outdoor activities and pleasures in the warmer months.

He'd passed a lake and boathouse, and what appeared to be a summer cottage or guest cottage, with ducks and swans gliding on a smaller pond beside it. The place looked serene, comfortable, with a wide terraced front, and from the sound he'd heard in the shady rear lawn, a couple of good-sized dogs to guard it.

Roger kneed the mount to a sedate walk, which took them under the arched entry and onto the brick road that would bring him to the front doors of the winged house. It curved to the right where the stables and other outbuildings stood.

He caught the movement as a groom exited the stable, wearing a wool coat, similar cap, thick trousers and knee-high boots. No livery here, he thought amused, but the typical local garments of wool and tweed and fisherman's sweater, and as he came closer, and took hold of the bit, that open smile and sea-marked face that branded his own servants.

"Good morning, my lord."

"Morning—?" Roger dismounted.

"Burton sir, ah, your lordship." The groom bowed. "Miss—er, Lady Joan said to expect you last week."

"Yes." Roger pulled off his gloves and untied his cape, still looking around. "I had a few things that required my attention and did not have time to make my apologies." He glanced at the man. "Is your mistress about?"

The man, who was around fifty years in age, nodded. His eyes shifted to the opening front door. "That would be Carver, the butler. Milord, I'll see to this fine beast. Welcome to Lecrox." He bowed.

Roger thanked him, feeling an odd sense of being scrutinized while he walked up to the front door. The butler was dressed, not surprisingly, as any London or estate butler would be, in stiff black and white. He had that straight-backed bearing and tall height that nearly put him even with Roger.

"Good morning, my lord. Welcome to Lecrox." The man bowed and then took Roger's cape and gloves, showing him into a foyer that was wood-paneled and warmed from the fires in the house.

"Good morning. Thank you," Roger said almost absently when he spied a plump woman dressed in a gray gown, snowy apron and cap standing a few feet away.

"I'm Agnes." She curtsied, her face wreathed in smiles and not at all hiding them. She hurried forward, and while he greeted her, Roger felt other eyes on him. Indeed, whilst following Agnes a moment later, he saw several maids and servants scurry away from doors and take off down halls.

He didn't know if he should be amused or mark it as strange, but he had the feeling that everyone was trying to get a look at him, and he'd vow, by the time he was in a back parlor with a glass of brandy-laced coffee that no less than three maids had come in, followed by two lads who'd tended the fires, and a housekeeper who looked him over as if judging horseflesh, whilst muttering she must get back to her duties, and her mistress would join him shortly.

When the last of them, *at least he hoped so*, was done entering and exiting, he sipped the drink which was very well done, and glanced around the room. The outer wall of windows was covered by royal blue drapes with gold tassels. They were the long ones he'd spied that would look out to the gardens. He was leaning by the mantle, but decided to walk around the room, remembering snippets of things Simon had relayed over the years about his uncle and the Lecrox household. Finding that relayed information fit well the understated elegance of the parlor, which he assumed was judged the most favored receiving room, by the servants that had put him there, considering they had treated him like royalty.

He scrutinized the white paneled walls, eyeing the richly framed art, again seeing taste rather than show. When he turned to make his way to the sofa, placed before the hearth, he took in marble-topped tables holding sometimes a piece of sculpture or a graceful lamp. Not until he sat, did he see the mantle and its grouping of silver candlesticks, framed portraits and snuffboxes. A simple oval mirror in silver hung above it. Interestingly, it seemed a seldom-used room.

Roger stood again, hearing the double doors click open, and turning to see Joan enter, not bothering to hide the fact that he liked the green velvet gown she wore. It had long sleeves and a low, square neckline, a style he'd already found flattering to her shape.

She wore an unadorned black choker and her hair was drying in those mussed curls around her head, looking a darker sable from the still-dampness. He knew them to be silky soft and was aware she thought them unattractive, but he did not.

He could see green high-heeled ankle boots when she walked toward him.

No, he thought again, Joan was no ravishing beauty, but she had presence and enough handsomeness to make him want to look at her often, and, he knew that under that gown, she was shaped perfectly feminine, and toned from being a physical woman. He tended to completely forget what another looked like when he was with her, feeling the silk and softness of her breasts, or kissing that graceful throat. *And no woman tasted as sweetly passionate as Joan.* None in his memory matched her for honest desire. *The way she looked at him*—it made him completely forget that others stared at his scarred face, or turned away from it. It was one of the reasons he avoided the debutante balls and vapid young women.

Joan had, on that first night she'd let herself explore him, kissed that side of his face and run her tongue over the damaged flesh.

"Hullo."

He nodded, surprised to hear the revealing husk in his tone when he offered regretfully, "I'm a bit late."

"A week." She smiled and waved him toward the sofa. "Would you rather move to the library?" her tone was dry. "I adore the servants, but they are a bit awed by your visit, and since my father died, quite excited to have a titled gentleman in the house."

Roger smiled and snorted. "The servant's grapevine must not be here, what it is in London."

She shook her head. "They keep up very well. It is simply that my father had a similar reputation to your own, before my mother wed him, and since they were very dear to him and vise versa, they pay not the least heed to it." She led the way out and down the hall to the library. "And," she said sliding the doors back, "they prefer um...real men...as opposed to some of the more foppish lords."

Roger followed her into the extensive room, instantly relaxing amid the leather furnishing and dark green décor. The walls were shelf upon shelf of books except for spaces where maps or hunt scenes, and one landscape was hung. There was a billiard table at the end, near the uncovered windows, and a stout, squat sideboard with decanters, glasses and spirits atop. Two fireplaces faced on opposite sides, one by the well-used desk and a grouping of comfortable, more masculine chairs. Here the tables were sturdy, the wood a warm rosewood hue. It was a space a tall man could move about with ease, as well as sit without straining the chair legs.

He watched Joan walk to the fireplace by the desk, before turning to regard him.

"Feel free to look around," she invited. "This was our favorite room in the house, Mother and Father and myself. We often played chess here after dinner, or read, sometimes merely sitting and talking." She waved to the other side of the room, "And playing billiards."

"It's a comfortable room." He scanned the shelves and then paused, staring at a painting that hung between built-in towers.

"My parents, Jordan and Anna," she told him.

Roger ambled over and lit a lamp on the side table, turning it up so it cast light on the painting. He stood back far enough to see the full effect. He knew without glancing over that Joan was watching him. He was aware simply from the way she spoke of them that she missed her parents, and had been close to them.

Perhaps in any other home, it would have seemed strange to see such a pose. But several things struck Roger as he eyed it. One was that Lord Jordan Lecrox was around his height and build, with lush sable hair and a face women would find extremely attractive. Another, was that his Anna was a beauty too, with almost white blond hair and deep blue eyes, petite and hour-glass shaped, with a smile that must have turned heads, and broken hearts for miles around. The third thing was the pose itself.

The couple was seated under an oak that he remembered seeing by the cottage, and Jordan was against the trunk, Anna between his legs, slightly on her side and, the man's arms were around her, her hands over his. There was an expression on their faces of complete confidence, a kind of inner knowledge, that they were where and whom they wanted to be, and confident in themselves. Not like the arrogant, richly dressed, down-your-nose portraits of his parents and ancestors. He'd wager too, that there was a twinkle in Jordan Lecrox's eye. He could see Joan was a mixture of their handsomeness, more favoring the strong bones from her father's blood, yet petite like her mother.

Joan's voice sounded softly amid his inner thoughts, "They passed much too early. It hardly seems fair, when someone finds happiness, when they are good, it seems wrong that they should have died."

He glanced at her. "How?"

"They were spending the Christmas holiday north, with a group of close friends. I'm not sure of the details, Agnes was here coddling me because of a slight fever. But the house where they were guests caught fire, and in the chaos Father refused to leave until every guest and servant was accounted for, and my mother refused to let him do the searching without her. It was a capricious thing, an explosion from the heat, that shattered some upper-story windows and injured my mother. The rest is speculation, but knowing Father, he tried to get her to safety and they died before he could." She shrugged. "They were together when found, embracing."

Roger glanced at the couple again, feeling the probable truth in that. He said, "I'm sorry, Joan."

"Thank you." She moved to the bar. "Now, would you like a brandy?"

"Yes." He strode slowly over to join her, watching her pour herself a finger before sitting on one of the chair-arms.

He sat on the edge of the desk, sipping and looking around before his eyes came to rest on her again. "I had to dash off to London," he told her.

"Something wrong?"

His smile was sardonic. "My cousin—the one who would be in line after me—it seems has sailed away in search of adventure, and left a letter with my solicitor stating his command that if I produced no heirs, the title would revert, since he has no interest in it."

"My. That spirit of adventure must run in your bloodlines."

Roger grunted. "Yes. I was under the impression he was a gentleman, as in ton standards. Earl immaculate compared to myself, so I was amazed. It seems he also sold off his holdings."

She took a sip of her drink, her eyes thoughtful, darker green he noted, from the hue of the gown she wore, and the colors in the room. She told him, as if musing aloud, "Your antipathy, is not because of the title, Roger, but rather those things that it reminds you of, and the ton's way of looking at it. You're a very good steward of your holdings."

"How do you know that?"

"Because, I judge by your personality, that you take your responsibility seriously. Your private life aside, or well, maybe not so private, since you do have a rep." She grinned. "I don't think your pride, nor your sense of self, would allow you to fail at anything."

Roger merely raised his brows and looked into the fire.

She said, "Even if you felt those things tied you down, prevented you from doing whatever, sailing the seas and captaining your ship, you know, deep in your bones, that you deserve the title, and that you are equal, if not better, than the past earl was."

He snorted. "My father, and many like him, would disagree."

"Your father may have been a man of arrogance, perhaps the very epitome of aristocracy, but any man who would cast off his own son without giving him a chance to explain, without wanting to hear differently if he did think the worst, is not a man of nobility, or of fairness. I'm sorry. But I see it this way—my parents knew the worst I had done, knew that I was ruined by society standards, and that I had made the most terrible mistake. Yet they loved me through their frustration, anger, hurt, their pain, likely at my defiance when they'd given me nothing but love and confidence. To look at what your parents did, even Maria, it does not reflect a mind, or a heart, that should be lord and master over anything."

Roger had not viewed it that way. *Of course, he had not.* But he had heard from Simon, seen and heard from her too, what a contrast there was in their upbringing. He knew the rigid way his father had looked at things, and expected nothing less. Perhaps a part of that younger man had hoped that his father would relent. But he had not, and there was a black bitterness in the reality of never having measured up or pleased the man.

He'd only recently admitted that he'd joined the war to get away from the constant tension and tyranny, from a man who on the one hand, wanted him to be a man, in his definition, and on the other, would never let him be, because he always had to be in control. He had to tear down and criticize and set impossible standards that even he himself had not adhered to. A man with a delusional image of himself, that Roger as a young man had finally found unbearable.

He finished off the drink on that last dark thought and set the glass down, asking and receiving permission to smoke. Lighting the cheroot he reflected on the combination that was Joan Lecrox. The mix of what he'd seen of her amid the ton, what he knew of her in private, intimate settings. And the kind of maturity she displayed now, when she talked about his past, without judgment of him. With observation, he supposed, and objectivity. He sometimes amazed himself at realizing how much he'd inadvertently revealed to her.

He had a secret from her, had lied to her once, with full knowledge of it. That week, after the first time, he had felt something, which he would not call jealousy, when she'd waltzed in the arms of other men, and when she conversed, stood near, or even looked at them. He was not possessive. He was not jealous. But once he *had* touched her, he could not picture another doing so, without wanting to beat them to a bloody pulp.

Roger cursed and pushed that feeling down as it tried to surface again. He did not know, as then, what he was expecting or what the relationship was evolving into. He only knew he was here, where she was, not raking and drinking and waking up in a blur of mixed images. He was not restless around her, merely he was often fascinated and hungry for her by turns.

"You're staring rather fierce."

He blinked. "Am I?"

"Yes. Narrowed eyes, and a nerve ticking in your cheek." She stood, smiling and setting her glass down before walking over to warm by the fire. "Finish your smoke, Wythe, so that I can trounce you in billiards."

Ah, he did like her humor. He laughed. "You sound sure of yourself."

She shot him a challenging smile. "I am."

Roger stood and pushed up his sweater sleeves, cigar in his white teeth. "Why wait? I'm quite ready."

She chuckled and proceeded to the billiard table.

Chapter 13

The mantle clock was ticking loudly. Joan had no idea what time it was, but they had partaken of dinner hours ago. Thus far, they were four games to six, and when Roger made the final victory shot, that put them four to seven, she sat down in one of the black leather chairs, and grunted, "I concede that you are the better player."

He set his cue stick in the rack and turned, lighting a cheroot before grinning at her. "And I concede that you are more challenging to beat than Simon."

She crowed at that, "I cannot wait to rub that in."

Roger sat in the opposite chair, sprawled and relaxed. The butler brought in coffee and smiled at them both.

"He trounced me," Joan told the man, knowing the servants had been slipping in, keeping track of the game.

"I'm sorry to hear that, milady." He poured the coffees, his eyes sliding from hers to Roger, while he suppressed a bigger smile. He handed Roger a cup saying soberly, "Lady Joan is very good at most sports."

"I'm sure she is." Roger shot her an amused smile. He too had noted the servants coming and going too often, hovering by the table.

"She used to play cards and billiards often with his lordship."

"Thank you." Joan nodded. "Now tell him, I won most of the time."

The butler made a sound and bowed to them both, muttering on his way out, "Agnes did not say to outright lie."

Joan was laughing as the door closed. She told Roger, "Do overlook them. They are trying to make me sound more interesting than I am, and, I think, more of a challenge."

Roger's brow raised. "It requires no effort on their part, Joan. You are both, in many ways that have nothing to do with sport, or games of chance."

"Ah, well, games of chance. Now there is a loaded phrase." She pretended to not be affected by his observation, all the while thinking, *he finds me interesting? Out of bed, with my clothing on interesting? He thinks me a challenge.* "Anyone who plays at games, takes a chance," she said, wondering at the implication that having had her he obviously still had not grown tired of the affair. That stirred some hope in her breast, however slim.

Roger lowered his cup, his sooty eyes moving over her face. He did make her flush, when he murmured low, in case her diligent servants were listening, "You took a chance that last day at Black Cross."

Joan swallowed, carefully placing her cup on the tray, not looking at him, she murmured, "The heat of the moment."

"Yes. But the risk of pregnancy remains a reality."

Her eyes jerked to his, and stayed there for an unmovable moment. A terrible feeling stuck in her midsection. "Is that why you are here? Why you said, you'd be here after…before the coach left?" Suddenly she could not breathe properly. He hesitated, and she blurted softly, "Of course it is. You did say that night at Co—"

"Joan—"

She stood in a jerky movement, walking to the fireplace to hide her expression, then forcing an even tone when she went on, "You said you'd marry me, should there be some result of our association."

"I meant that." He had stood too, and was walking toward her. Standing a foot away when she turned.

Joan had her hands behind her back, her fingers tight together. "You don't think I'd hold you to that, do you? You don't imagine that I would extract some price for what you—"

"Christ, Joan. We're not talking about price and payment. But rather the mature decision we made."

"If we should get caught?"

"It is more than that, if you are pregnant." He stared her. "You're an adult, we are, both mature here."

She made herself smile. "Yes, we are. And as an adult, I'll deal with whatever comes from my decisions. Or my impulses."

He tossed the cheroot into the fire, walking close enough to look down at her, to tilt her chin up so that she had to meet his gaze. "If there is a child, you will know, when?"

"In a month or so—"

"And you will tell me." He waited, then as she said nothing, he insisted firmer, "Joan, you will tell me."

"Yes." Her voice was strained. She moved his hand away, looking into the fire. "I will let you know."

Behind her he said with soft steel, "No, you won't. You are just stubborn enough not to."

"What I am is sure there is nothing to worry about. What I am not, is a woman who would trap a man into marriage."

"No one has stated that. It was a mutual thing, Joan, and I could have stopped at any point."

She closed her eyes, feeling him looking at her while he stood behind her. "I'll let you know."

The clock ticked, the fire crackled, and her eyes opened, but she did not turn to face him again, and he did not speak for too many long, drawn-out moments.

She stiffened only a second, when his hand touched her nape, before it rested on the back of her head. Standing so close, she could smell him, feel his heat, he muttered huskily, "Even with that between us, I am thinking of where in this bloody house of over-protective servants I could coax you into a tryst."

Joan was torn between laughter and some deep soreness. He was here simply because of that last time, *not* because he wanted to court her, or be around her on some other level. Laughter won out, somewhat self-mocking, because, a thousand times today, she had wanted him. A bloody million times, during that billiard game she'd watched his face, watched his body move, caught his eye, and melted inside with need.

She ultimately turned and raised her arms, until they were around his neck, standing on tiptoe, offering her mouth.

He lowered his head and took it.

The kiss was unhurried, yielding, yet it brought that same hum of awareness and stirred the same greed. His hands were splayed on her back and his lips held that familiar magic that stole her breath, while his tongue stirred deeper fires and secret hungers. She would never get used to the things he did with that tongue, the way his mouth felt inside, and the way kissing him made her feel.

Roger lifted his head, his hands low on her spine. He murmured, "We should marry anyway, Joan. These times are but a taste, and there has been no lingering, no opportunity for more than the bare minimum." He pulled her to him, his husk revealing, "Christ…I want more. More than one time, more than twice, and more bloody time to touch, and taste you the way I have not yet."

With her cheek against his heart, feeling the hard thud, Joan fought temptation, the serious kind that wanted her to say yes, to take advantage of his physical desire for her, to give her heart ease. But in the core of her, she could not live with that, not even to have him for her own, any time she wanted.

"I thought you refused to come back to Black Cross, because we'd slipped up," he murmured quietly.

"No." Her tone was quiet. "I discovered that you were correct, the craving only builds, and losing one's control is rather sobering." She sighed. "Not that I have control otherwise." Her laugh was less convincing. "But I did not care at that moment what happened next. That kind of recklessness is not befitting a mature woman, supposedly making circumspect decisions."

He rubbed his chin lightly against her hair, saying low, "Perhaps, I've gone from a rake to a cad for tempting you into this affair. If I had known—"

"What?"

"Nothing," he growled softly. "I would have still wanted you." He lowered his head and ran his tongue over her ear before nibbling below it and whispering, "I still would have seduced you."

"You take too much responsibility." She arched her neck for his kisses. "The decision was mine." Joan moaned when he suckled a sensitive spot. "I still want you, too."

Roger had bent his knees and was kissing across the top of her breasts, muttering that the neckline was not low enough to access him what he sought.

Joan felt enough of that intensity in him, to know he was swiftly losing himself in the objective—*to get her into bed.* In the next instant it was she who said on a moan, "I suppose I could slip you above stairs, into my bed."

He paused, straightened, and looked down at her. "You would do that, here?"

"I've taken many chances to be with you Roger."

He cupped her face, his thumbs stroking her cheeks. "I know that, Joan." He stared at her for a moment, apparently lost in mental thoughts, before he whispered, "You once told me that you would not wed without intimacy. Do I give you that?"

"Yes."

He let his thumb play at the corner of her mouth. "You give me much too, Joan. More than I had anticipated." He went on, "We would do well in a marriage. I know, that I suggested it early in our association, to deal with any scandal on your part. But I've never asked nor thought to wed another. I will not."

"You do not have to wed me, to have me, Roger. I'm no longer fooling myself. We're having an affair."

"As I was saying." He put his thumb over her lips and winked. "It seems I must wed, and must have an heir, and I

144

cannot think of another woman whom I would care to offer either to. I'm offering it here, now, Joan. Will you marry me?"

Already weak in the knees, she stared into those dark, watchful eyes, feeling something in his question that was more than the words. Again, she was torn, because she knew he had not, would not, offer it to another, she knew him that well. He would not tie himself to any ton deb or any society woman. And part of her kept saying, that none of those women would ever take the time to understand him, to know him, and see anything of him below the surface. They would wed him for wealth and title and none of them would love him the way she did, or love him, simply for himself.

"And when you tire of me?" she could not help but ask. *Weak, weak, Joan.*

He rubbed her lip again. "I don't think I will."

She laughed and closed her eyes, drawing in a deep breath. "You will. But I am fool enough to want you, until you do."

When she opened her eyes, his brow was cocked curiously. "Does that mean yes, or no?"

Joan's mind called her a bloody fool, but the man was touching her, looking at her, and what could she do, but say, "Yes. I will."

He smiled slowly and drew her into his arms, kissing her a long time, stealing her breath, before the sound of a cleared throat brought them apart.

"We're going to be married," Roger told the butler who stood just inside the door, mostly because Joan was holding him, trying to gain her composure.

The man smiled and blinked. "Ver—ah, very good, sir, uh… milord." He bowed and nearly fell over his feet going out the door.

Laughing breathlessly, Joan said, when Roger turned to her, "The news will reach London by dawn. Agnes will have it all over Bristol in the next hour."

"No doubt." He asked then, "Who will give you away?"

"Uncle Willy." Her smile was dry. "He'll do it most gladly. He's made it his mission since he cannot get Simon to toe the mark, that I should be the one to uphold the traditions in the family."

"I recall you did the season for him?"

"Yes. And he was not happy I quit before an announcement."

"Then he'll be too pleased to do the honors on short notice."

Roger walked over and collected his jacket.

"I thought you were sneaking into my bed tonight?" Joan watched him pull it on with some dismay, and not a little sexual frustration.

"It will be our bed, after the wedding." He winked. "I've a special license to acquire and a few missives to write. I shall need a few things from London and to contact our solicitors." Roger walked over to where she sat, on the arm of the chair, and touched her cheek. He was a bit more serious when he searched her face this time. "Are you sure?"

"You should ask yourself that," she said, "since you do not have to wed me."

"I'm not a man to make light promises. I make very few in fact. I think we both know what we are getting. But you will, in becoming the Countess of Wythe, find yourself, the object of speculation and gossip. You will have to do the season, at least in part. I want your eyes open, when you take my name."

She read something that gave her pause in his eyes, but not enough to turn him down twice. "They're open," she whispered and thought on a sigh, *they bloody well are, and it still apparently does not matter to my heart.*

He kissed her temple and offered before departing, "You do whatever is required on your end, and I shall call in two days with the details."

146

"Lucky for me, I still have a few gowns that will suite for a bride." She called that out with forced humor.

At the doorway Roger supplied, "It's you I'll want, Joan, it matters not a whit if you're dressed or not."

Joan watched that door close and muttered, "Yes, well, there is that, Wythe. Which is exactly why we're both bloody fools."

Chapter 14
The Wedding Day, Lecrox Manor

Uncle Willy, the Earl of Collingsworth, gave Joan away. Dressed in deep claret and smiling from ear to ear at her, he was a man of sixty-eight years and wore a close cropped beard. At one time, his hair was the shade of his son's, but now was completely white. He could not stop shaking Wythe's hand and, rep aside, there was no doubt he welcomed him into the family. In fact Roger got the distinct impression that Uncle Willy thought this some reformation on his part, which would ultimately rub off on Simon, a notion Roger should have banished for the man since Simon looked in no state to learn any lessons from the event.

But the earl did have a care for Joan, and for that Roger was willing to play any sort of role that gave them both happiness today. He was still somewhat reeling from the difference in which the Lecrox servants treated him. They'd gone all out for the wedding.

Simon, who stood as best man, during a ceremony with only the staff and parish priest present, showed not the least bit of surprise at being summoned for a wedding at less than two weeks notice. Then again, Joan was not sure if it was because his eyes had only just cleared to sobriety after being pumped full of black coffee by his father and Roger the day of arrival. He did have to be nudged by both Roger and the priest to hand over the ring, and there was a pause whilst he tried to recall where he'd put it. Thankfully it turned out to be where it should be—in his breast pocket.

But much later, having a cigar and drink with Roger in his uncle Jordan's study, he looked out at the first falling snow flakes, and swirled the brandy in his glass saying, "I don't know how the bloody hell it all got by me."

Roger had heard that for the past two days, and he grinned, half-seated on the desk and watching Simon by

148

the French doors. "I can be discreet when the occasion demands it."

"She's m'cousin and all but, to get leg-shackled. Good God." Simon shook his head. "I thought you were as skeptical as myself about that nonsense."

When Simon turned to look at him, Roger's smile was secretive. "It takes the right woman, the right circumstances, and the right twist of fate, to change your mind."

"If you say so. But not me." Simon shuddered and knocked back the brandy. "Fine for you two I suppose, but there's too few like m'cousin out there. Besides, other than sex, what on earth do you need them for?"

Roger opened his mouth, but a knock sounded on the door.

Joan poked her head in, spying Simon and winking at him. She looked back at Roger. "The minister is leaving. I thought perhaps you'd like to see him off."

"Yes." Roger straightened, watching her walk into the room. She was wearing a champagne silk gown, with snug sheer sleeves and scoop bodice. It fit her like a glove. He'd been itching to feel the thing ever since he'd spied her coming down the stairs before the ceremony. She'd been giving him such hungry looks since then, that he was damned anxious to at last, have all the time they wanted together.

Joan strode over and helped herself to a sip of his drink before he set it down. Meeting his eyes she muttered, "It has been six days, two hours, and twenty minutes since I touched you. I'm thinking of tying you to the bed, and keeping you there."

He laughed low but his eyes leapt with hungry flames. Bloody hell, he was going to enjoy being wed to her. He kissed her and murmured back, "I'm sporting, in fact, I'll supply neck-cloths."

When he'd left, Joan blew out a breath, polished off the rest of the brandy, shuddering before she turned to Simon.

His long hair tied back, neat cravat lasting only as long as the *I will*, and now in his shirtsleeves, he looked like he'd just crawled out of a bottle.

"You are not upset, that I took your rakehell friend out of commission for a while, are you?"

"No. Not at all, puss." He smiled slightly and shook his head, coming over to kiss her temple then refilling his glass. "I'm amazed however, that he's gotten himself leg-shackled."

She mumbled, "It amazes me too." But then said honestly, "I will make him very happy, Simon. I'll make him laugh, and I'll love him better than those who had the chance and refused to."

He stared at her a long time, his eyes not leaving hers, and for once, being just as serious. "I believe that you will."

Roger came back in, glancing at the two. He said to Simon, "Your father is leaving. You're welcome to stay longer, but my wife and I won't be available to entertain you."

"That's quite all right." Simon laughed as Roger took Joan in his arms. "I'm off to Scotland for a month of drinking and raking."

Roger raised his head from kissing Joan. He met Simon's last look back, by the door. He pulled her to him, resting his chin atop her head and said, "My thanks, Simon, for rushing down and standing up with me."

Simon grunted, smiled dryly, shook his head and shut the door saying, "I had to see it to believe it."

Joan, snug in his embrace, waited until the house quieted, then stepped back enough to stand on her tiptoes and whisper, "I'll take that cravat now."

He put her hands on the silky material, his eyes lustrous with inner heat. "I trust you will allow me to return the favor?"

She took the cloth and wrapped it around one of his wrists, smiling wickedly. "I found these amazing oils in one of those secret drawers last week, whist we were going over those papers with your solicitor. I'll let you pay me back when we're there again."

"Joan," Roger laughed on a groan, "I should have wed you sooner."

"We were pressed for time before, and had to be careful. I had to worry about being seen, and those were stolen hours." She flashed her wedding ring. "This changes things. Unless you intend to dash off in the next week or so."

"I have made a dozen plans," his lashes dipped, "and all of them consist of one or the both of us being nude and preferably, not leaving the bedroom."

She whispered, "I'm sure we'll make it up the stairs eventually. But I've found that removing the limits on our um…adventures, even mentally, has opened my imagination to all sorts of wickedly seductive scenarios."

He stared at her. "I like the sound of that."

Joan laughed. But in her mind, for the past two weeks, were her own plans, and while being nude and in bed played a big role in them, she'd also had time to think of exactly what had made her fall in love with this man, and, what she had a chance to give him, that no other could. She'd scraped up some wisdom and found herself sifting through what she knew of him, and what she thought he really needed from her. Not just sexually, but the kind of partner he could always be honest, and be himself, with. She had missed him, wanted him, hungered for him as much as he did her. She intended to make his wedding night one to remember. One that he would never regret.

She'd undone his shirt and was now working on his trousers. Roger felt the silk slip over his other wrist, before she led him to the shelf, and slipped the ends around the sturdy ladder rung above his head. Next she was floating downward and he felt her breathe on his skin, warm enough to speed his heart a dozen times faster. He moaned from the warm lave of her tongue as it touched the sensitive tip of his sex. Roger shuddered from the thought and surprise that she wanted to, that she was, and that this was the Joan he'd had to coax into exposing her limbs that first night.

His head went back, his knees weak, his mind filled with deep red and mists of erotic vapor. "Joan...Joan..." he husked in the shadows discovering once more, that she had the keen ability to arouse him so intensely.

Her sound of pleasure echoed up to him, as her palms slid up his hips.

But he was lost in a haze of carnal bliss when her mouth took him fully. The thought of it set his blood on fire, never mind that her inner mouth felt like liquid silk. For once he wasn't aware of what he was saying, but he was pretty damned sure it was explicit. Whatever it was that drew from the feeling and knowledge of what she was doing, it came in guttural growls from his lips.

The moment he released with a thousand infinitesimal flames, his mind drifted somewhere above his body. He was beyond thought for several extended moments. Roger rumbled her name in that daze, straining at the bonds. He recalled little else, until she was reaching up and releasing him.

He'd half latched his trousers and reached for her, kissing her fully, deeply before pulling back to look at her. "That was on your mind before tonight? In your fantasies?"

"Yes." She soothed her swollen mouth.

Roger watched that action and said, "I thought you were jesting earlier."

"No. Did it feel like a jest?"

"Hell, no." He stared into her eyes. Then said, "You were too good, love."

She covered his hands and grinned. "Instinct, I assure you."

"You bloody well have exemplary ones, then." He kissed her again. "Ring for some coffee while I wash up. Have the maid bring it to your rooms."

"We can use the master chambers."

"So long as there is a bed, on second thought, I don't actually care if there is a bed or not."

Chuckling she returned. "Go, on to my rooms. I'll see to the coffee."

An hour later, they reclined on Joan's bed, atop the champagne silk coverlet, having sipped strong coffee and stripped off their clothing.

Roger insisted on a lamp, even though the fireplace was ablaze and lit the room sufficiently.

Joan was fairly sure, that there wasn't a spot of skin on her frame that he had not looked over the past hour, and rather intently too. She occupied her own eyes, having only seen him this way, that one time in London. At the moment her hand was on his muscled flank, caressing the lightly-haired area, and enjoying the heat as well as the strength in them.

He was propped on his elbow beside her, his hand splayed over her right breast.

"Did you look over the papers carefully, before you signed them?" he asked quietly.

Joan lifted her lids to glance upwards. "Yes. You left Lecrox and my inheritance in my name." She ran her hand further up, near his groin. "You didn't have to. I trust you not to squander it away."

"I don't need your wealth, Joan. I also think you're capable of running it yourself. I believe your parents wanted that."

"Thank you."

His fingers flexed on her breast because she was getting closer to his aroused flesh.

"I think the solicitor was nearing heart failure at your protestations over the title."

"I made the concession," Joan said dryly. "I can tolerate being called my lady, and countess, so long as I can still be myself. I have a title and used it in London, but I think of myself as I am here."

He grunted on a laugh, "I can't imagine, outside the ton, that you would do otherwise."

"Nor you." She rolled to face him, her hand now on his hip. "I'm keenly interested, by the way, in getting to…ah...know you better."

Roger's lips curved when her hand slid down to fist him. His hand covered hers and removed it. He leaned, to roll her onto her back, and gaze down at her.

His voice held a rasp when he murmured, "I've no objections in general, but I've a very secret mission to accomplish first." He kissed her lips, then slid down to tease her nipples until she was moaning. Taking his time, he suckled each breast and ignored her tugging his hair and arching under him. He laved his way across her ribs, down her midsection and at last dipped his head so that he could taste her tangy essence.

"Roger!"

He bit lightly at the tender inside of her groin, murmured something against her skin, and then parted her curls for the flat of his tongue.

Joan's gasps and groans echoed the pleasure he gave her in the subsequent half-hour. He laved, suckled, and kissed her exposed flesh until she was covered in a faint sexual mist and begging for release.

When her entire body vibrated, coupled with her tugging more aggressively on his hair, Roger raised his head and whispered, "Yes, let go now love, give us both pleasure." Then he put his tongue on her again, applying enough pressure and friction so that she climaxed loud and long, her muscles jerking and flexing with every delve of his tongue.

Joan was panting softly, breathing shallow, when he covered her, holding his weight up, while he kissed her, and mingled her scent with the taste of their mouths.

She lifted her heavy lids and even with her eyes shimmering with moisture from the intensity of the climax, she could still see his onyx eyes and swarthy face, still read the desire there. "I shall likely *never* get used to that incredible feeling. You take me out of my skin and my head, with that beautiful mouth."

He touched it to hers before raising again. "As you did me earlier." His body shifted to lie between her legs. "It is my pleasure to kiss that part of you, which welcomes me so eagerly inside." He flexed his hips, sliding only an inch into her.

Joan's breath caught, she said tightly, "Each time before, when we did this, I ached to have you stay inside me. I hated that we were rushed. I felt empty when your body left mine."

Muscles tensely held, he ground softly, "There is no time, no hour, no need for parting tonight." He surged deep, filling her completely, groaning against the pillow when her thighs lifted and held him tightly. "Christ, love, you feel so good."

She placed her hands on his upper arms and lifted her hips. "So do you."

Roger elevated enough to lift the bulk of his weight from her, yet positioned himself for long steady thrusts. The sounds then, amid the harsh breaths and soft moans, were half whispers stolen by a gasp, cut off by the flames raging higher.

He kept a steady pace, a powerful cadence that forced her to hang on tightly. His muscles shifted, his body moved with feral grace and earthy sagacity, stroking her with voracity, a dominance that was also bent on pleasing. He had to halt eventually and gather his control.

Roger looked down at her, his brow damp and face tense. "Too much, love?"

"No." She wet her lips. Sliding her hands up his back. "I'm marveling at your control, Roger. This feels too glorious."

He laughed, strained and muttered, "It does. And it's slipping by the second."

Joan arched her neck and moved her fingertips to his hard nipples and abraded them. Seeing his lashes dip with pleasure, she curled in so that she latched onto them with her mouth and suckled.

Roger cursed, then groaned before he began thrusting swift and hard. When his climax was upon him, he moaned, "Your instincts, love, are going to be the death of us both."

~

A long soak in a steaming tub was Joan's only request after two similar tests of Roger's restraint. She lay in frothy suds, watching him as he slept, sprawled face down on the bed, having not bothered with drying off after his own ablutions.

He'd bathed in the master chambers. She'd been sitting there in the tub when he'd come through, bare-arsed, and fallen across the sheets. No lamp turned up now, but the relaxing glow from the fire lit the quiet room.

Joan was too filled with emotions to sleep. She really should pinch herself, she thought, eyeing that tanned, masculine form. She not only had Wythe for a lover, he was her husband as well. *Now, if only she could have his heart.*

Joan sighed and sank under the water, washing her hair before slicking it back. Life was going to intrude eventually. After the holiday, they must tour his estates and that, she assumed would mean busy days and too-short nights. Then came the season, which they would face as man and wife, earl and countess. She did not underestimate the ripples of shock that likely went through society at their union. Poor Simon was still reeling no doubt, and muttering into his brandy glass.

Half the haute ton were probably asking who the bloody hell Joan Lecrox was. She had heard of Wythe before she'd met him, and did not relish, now that she loved him, wondering which of those attractive fashionable females he'd slept with over the years.

She sat up and braced her hands on the rim, standing and slicking the suds from her tummy and limbs, leaning over to collect her towel.

"You won't need that, love."

Joan glanced at the bed, seeing Roger lying on his back, hands folded behind his head and magnificently aroused.

"I thought you were asleep."

"I was." He slid up further and raised one knee, lazily letting his gaze trace her shimmering wet body. "Are you feeling any effects?"

Her brow rose.

"Are you sore?"

"No." She flushed and tossed the towel on the floor, stepping out on it. "But I'm getting chilled."

He eased off the bed, giving her a thrill as he strode to the fireplace, shoving his mussed hair back behind his ears, and turning to beckon her over.

Curious, already feeling the glow from his look, she padded to him, and glanced up, waiting.

He caught her under the arms and lifted her, saying, "Wrap your legs around me."

She did, now wet where it mattered most, felt the best, and filling herself with his flesh easily. She held on.

Teeth sank into his lip, he lifted and lowered her, letting her discover all sorts of new sensations from the position. In fact Joan was so excited, she had no idea she was saying so, until he stopped and laughed helplessly.

"What?" Her eyes were wide.

"Nothing." He kissed her, still smiling. "I am just discovering that I should never count on having any control whatsoever around you."

"Oh. Why not?"

"Because." He leaned his head back a moment. Then lowered it. "You do not pretend or fake your response. Because you are open to everything and you're bloody enthusiasm for me, robs everything else from my mind."

"Then we're equal, because I do not even try to think when you feel this good." She leaned in for a kiss, murmuring against his lips. "Let me down."

He did, however with a frown of regret.

She led him to the bed, pushed him down, and eased down on his flesh again.

Joan waited for his hands to settle on her hips before she began to undulate and lift and lower herself. Feeling the sparks up her spine, she husked, "I like looking at you, being able to see you."

He slid his hands up and cupped her breasts, eyes flaming between his lowered lashes he rasped, "The view is equally as pleasing for me."

She sped her movements and watched him struggle, before he gave up control and began to arch with her, to close his eyes and sink into the pleasure. When he was at the end of his tether she reached back and scored the bunched muscles lining his thighs lightly with her nails.

"Joan!" His body bowed, shuddered and trembled.

Joan closed her own eyes, absorbing the power of it into her, feeling again the soothing scorching of his seed.

~

For two months the weather fluctuated between icy rain and snow. On the days that flakes piled into drifts, Joan rode with Roger, sometimes to the church if they were at Lecrox that week, or vise versa if they were not. On the rainy, dreary days, they played billiards, chess, or cards, and spent time in their respective offices, doing estate work.

158

As she mentally predicted, it didn't take the Lecrox servants long to warm to Roger. They positively spoiled him. Joan was amused when his favorite meals were cooked more often than her choice, and his coffee served the way he liked, as well as at the footmen and maids, who sometimes hovered wherever he was, to do his least bidding.

Joan heard him, at night, murmuring about the vigilant servants she employed. But she noticed that he lingered to talk to the groom, and that he winked and teased Agnes to blushes, as well as being allowed in cook's domain when he felt like it, something even she was scolded for.

They had ultimately moved into the large master suite, after Roger had her store her parents' things, and moved a few pieces from Black Cross. Joan silently thanked him for his perception, because those rooms and possessions were so closely linked with her parents, she had been unable to make the transformation herself.

But with the different furnishings and dark gold and blue fabrics, it became their bedchamber, more after Roger added his personal items to her own.

Black Cross became a place they explored and worked, once they realized she was not yet pregnant. Joan enjoyed dressing in her trousers, handing Roger tools or oiling wood, or simply polishing the fixtures. The servants there too, were gracious and friendly. It was with some dread that Joan marked the day they would have to tour Wythe's holdings, due to the fact that he'd already given her an impression that though rich and opulent, the estates and servants were rigidly cold and formal. Sometimes as they worked at Black Cross, she'd cautiously bring up his father and his early life, and the hints that he did drop were so abrupt and terse, that she nothing but dreaded that they should ever have to be go back to anything linked to them.

And, having talked, laughed and made love with Roger over the past two months, Joan regrettably saw a notable change in him as their trunks were packed with their formal clothing, and the coach was readied for their journey.

She stood by the window watching the drizzle melt the last of the snow. Today she'd dressed carefully in a gold gown and wore matching topaz jewelry on her hands, ears, and neck. Agnes had laid out her fur muff and sable-trimmed cloak. In her side vision, Roger was pulling on a black jacket over his white silk shirt. He'd had three inches cut from his hair the previous evening.

"Ready?"

She turned and skimmed his frame, finding him wonderfully virile in the formal black and white, noting that his neck-cloth matched her gown, and the stickpin held the same design as his signet ring. His hair was brushed straight back and tied with a black cord.

"You look very handsome."

He smiled, but only with his mouth. Roger walked to the bed and picked up her coat and muff, handing them to her and saying, "Gold is as ravishing on you as green."

Already knowing he preferred her in that color, she walked out and down the stairs with him, ignoring the fact he'd said it with preoccupation. Tensely seated in the well-sprung coach, Joan mentally dreaded every mile that moved them away from the closeness of Lecrox and Black Cross.

Chapter 15

For Joan, the weeks were a strain more for Roger than herself. She could play the countess, and did so, choosing to ignore the haughty servants. She set it in her mind to enjoy the exquisite art and expensive décor in each of the households. Perfection was subjective, she mused, but the old earl and countess certainly aimed for it with no expense spared. The chefs were the foremost, never mind that they so rarely had to cook for the earl. The finest quality of fabrics graced windows and bedchambers and sitting rooms. She did try *not* to pace while Roger met with stewards and secretaries, and when he made it to dinner, she discussed anything *but* where they were, and whom they were as far as the servants were concerned.

But the nights were telling—once the day ended and Roger was through handling problems, dealing with stewards and checking on tenants. After his bath, he became restless, brooding and quiet, and too many times she found him in the portrait gallery, looking up at the paintings of his parents. And, too many times Joan wanted to scream and rail at their ghosts, because no matter how old he was now, and what he had accomplished, there was still that young man in him who had not only failed to please his father, but who'd received the ultimate wound to carry through life. They had died having not spoken to him in years. It was only through the solicitor that she'd learned his father had not intended to pass the title to Roger, that the untimely death was the only thing that had kept his signature off those papers. She did not understand a man who would do that simply because of rumor. Moreover, she suspected that it may have had nothing to do with the war or Roger's role, but the fact that he'd left home and dared to have his own life.

The servants did not help with their stiffness and distance. Joan was no simpleton, she knew good and well they echoed the snobbery and arrogance of the past earl.

That no matter if Roger was faultless, they did not feel him equal to his father. Too many of them, she suspected from their age, likely bore that smug look she'd sometimes witnessed, by virtue of his London rep. No doubt that added weight to his father's ridiculous condemnation. If it was her choice, *she'd let them all go, and good riddance.* But this was her husband's domain, and they were his ghosts to banish.

Stifled, suffocated in the gilt and richness, the very coldness of the house, Joan welcomed the last week and the coming of spring, by slipping out of the mansion at noon, and walking in the gardens. Buds were not yet showing, yet the carefully kept statues and benches gave an impression that, in full bloom, it would be breathtaking. Today, however she sought a different kind of atmosphere, one in which she could clear her head and rid herself of the misgivings that were weighing heavily on her. Roger had not been intimate with her in weeks.

Joan was mature enough to realize that the long hours and mental demands, along with his complete dissatisfaction with being there, contributed to his aloofness. This was the main house he'd lived in with them, been tutored in, and she comprehended, been under the wrath of a father, who was either a tyrant or coldly cutting. Of his mother, she could judge from the portrait that the woman lacked both spirit and indeed, any strong emotion, including love. She didn't appear brow-beaten, but rather detached in expression. The both of them were dressed rich as royalty in those oversized paintings. Like the homes it reeked of self-importance and the materialistic ostentation was somewhat stifling.

The Roger she knew would not welcome her verbalizing her summations, Joan thought. Consequently, it put her in a tense position. She hated seeing him shut down and she could not stand that he had no way to vent or express what he felt. *She would almost rather that he lashed out at her.* Anything, but that contained discipline.

And those black frowns, which served him well here, and amid the ton, but not as a husband to a woman who was trying bloody hard to share his burdens.

Joan whiled away an hour before hearing the secretary, Sir Alfred depart. She arose from the bench, and strolled to the French doors that were thrown open, seeing Roger standing by the unlit fireplace smoking a cheroot.

She sighed and said loud enough. "The sun is out today."

"Umm." He turned and glanced at her, blowing a stream of smoke.

Joan tilted her head. "I thought I'd strip nude and walk around the garden."

Hand on the cigar, he paused and slowly pulled it from his lips. "What did you say?"

She laughed. "I said I'm going to pull my gown off and run around the garden stark naked."

For the first time in weeks his lips twitched, and then curved into a smile.

Something light bloomed in her chest, and she felt like weeping with joy because she'd made that smile appear. "Do you think that's a good idea?"

"If you wish to give the staff heart failure, by all means."

"Actually, that is good idea. They need a shock or two." Her mouth turned down in a comical frown. Then she wiggled her brows. "Care to add your bare bum to the act? We could stand on that monstrous fountain and yell obscenities."

"Joan." He was laughing now.

She laughed with him, and then went on lightly, "Did Roger the Rakehell lose his virtue here?"

He snorted, "The only thing that was stiff in this house, were my parents, and the servants."

She giggled then, "Where did you launch your uh...carnal education?"

He sat down on the chair arm, looking at her but apparently thinking. "When I did the tour...a group of us chaps went together."

"And?" She leaned her head back against the door smiling.

"And," he shrugged, "they were panting after some silly chit with an affected lisp, while I was being seduced by an actress."

"Seduced?" She raised her brows. "What was she like?"

"I don't recall."

"Oh come now, you must remember something."

He slid back in the chair, one leg still over the arm while he drew on the cheroot thoughtfully. After blowing a stream of smoke, he supplied, "Nipples."

Laughter spewed for a moment, and Joan put her hand to her mouth, eyes dancing, even when she prodded, "Nipples?"

"That's all I remember. She had miniature breasts but impressive nipples."

"Is that better?"

His own brow went up but his smile was there. "I've no idea. You're prodding a vague memory, and no, I don't recall her name."

"Just her nipples." Joan laughed. "How fascinating."

He narrowed his eyes, smiling a bit wider. "You're in a fit mood."

She ignored that. "So, you recalled her nipples, and what about others?"

"Other breasts?"

"No, other women."

"You want to know this rot?"

"Yes. It's just conversation, and vastly more interesting than cows and sheep. Now tell me, who came next."

"I don't know the order, Joan."

"Mmm."

"There was a dancer with long legs, incredible flexibility." His dark eyes twinkled.

"I heard that somewhere, that they were, likely from Simon in his cups." She grinned. "Did you keep a mistress?"

"Yes, on and off."

"What were they like?"

"Expensive and bitchy," he uttered succinctly.

She looked around the interior. "You should have done it in here."

"Your wits are twisted today."

She snorted. "At least you'd have some personal memory tied to the place that was not mirthless. In fact..." Her eyes met his guarded ones. "I'm willing to participate in creating one."

He stared at her.

Joan felt a breeze ruffle her hair and wished she had not mentioned the trepidation of the place.

She pressed onward gruffly, "Would you do something for me?"

"In your present mood, I hesitate to say yes."

Her lashes lowered. "Would you lock that inside door and take your clothing off?"

He tossed the cigar in the hearth and sat up, looking at her for a long a time.

"I'll keep watch. No one will see you but me."

"What is your point in having me do that?" His tone was tight.

Softly she supplied, "You trust me, don't you?"

"Most of the time," he murmured. "Today, I am not so sure."

"I'd never hurt you knowingly, in any way, Roger. I'd never initiate anything that would make you feel at a disadvantage."

He sat there scrutinizing her so long that Joan was starting to feel anxious that she'd pushed too far, perhaps. But he did rise, and did walk to the interior door and lock it. He was beyond the sunlight streaming through, standing in the shade of the corner, although visible when he began unbuttoning his pristine, white shirt.

He pulled it free and wide. Her heart hammered in her ears. Joan watched him discard his boots, release his hair, and when only in trousers, their eyes met a moment, while his hands were applied at the closures over his groin.

She wet her lips watching his hair slide forward, waved from being tied back. The scar on his face stood out from the tense set of the sinew. Heat bloomed and spread under her skin when he was standing there, completely nude, more real and better-forged than any statue in the garden, ardently splendid amid the richness of his surroundings.

"You're a beautiful man," she said honestly, "There is nothing in this room, in this house, in this world, that compares. "

He was silent, his stance relaxed but his eyes hooded.

"There is only one thing your parents did that I am grateful for and that is having you. And there are many good things that came from them driving you away, and from Maria's stupidity. And the best of it, is that I met you, and you became my lover, and now you are my husband." She slowly pulled away from the door and pushed it closed. Holding his gaze while she walked toward him, she added in a hushed voice, "And I want you...I want to touch you, here, anywhere, all of the time."

He did not resist when she reached out and took his hand, walking back until they were in the squares of sunlight radiating through the French doors. She began to undress then, tossing first her blouse and then her skirt onto a nearby chair. She removed all but her silk stockings, and knelt, pulling him down on the thick carpet. She kissed his lips only once, before she moved to his feet.

Joan began to touch him, to map him from ankle to thigh with her palms and mouth. The sun was warm, almost too vivid, but she hardly noticed when she skimmed over swarthy flesh and muscle, and shaped sinew with her hands. She let her eyes follow her motions, missing nothing, attending every hollow and bulge. He became aroused. She kept kissing, touching, stroking, over the tender flesh below his navel, up that ridged stomach.

Lingering on the dusky, pebbled nipples, Joan went down each arm, conscious that her breathing was heavy, and unsteady too, stirred by the parts of her skin that touched his.

She urged him onto his stomach, watching him press his forehead into his folded arms, before she started her expedition again, nipping at his spine, tracing up it, between the hard, fanned muscle of his back. She saw his chills, heard his deep sound when her tongue traced over the slope of his buttock, and detected a rumble of pleasure when her teeth scraped the underside and indented sides.

She smoothed her hands over his thighs and calves, kissing the bend of his knees, then making the journey of kisses and laves and nibbles back up.

Seated lightly astride him, she moved his hair aside at the nape, and kissed him there, murmuring when he gave her more access, then reaching to turn his face to the side, so that she could suckle below his ear and nip at his rigid jaw.

Joan was half over him when he turned, and looking down, laying atop him so that her breath caught when those sunbeams struck his eyes. Though his thick sooty lashes were lowered, she could see enough of the pupils, to catch the glitter of sienna streaks glinting from the center.

His hands came up to skim her back, and instantly forced her head down for a kiss that needed no words to relay his desire.

Roger smoothly switched their positions, and filled her with his flesh in an aggressive thrust. She had to jerk her mouth free, and fill her lungs, but it caught once more as Roger began to move in her. Crying out, she sucked in an insufficient breath and absorbed his solid submersion. He was breathing tensely, rhythmically, lifting, keeping her legs high and wide, wanting deep penetration and succeeding to the point that she moaned with each rough collision. She realized that it was raw emotion. She did not care. Joan reveled in every second that ensued, every harsh sound that came from his lungs, and each forceful thrust of his sex. It was rapid, but immensely eloquent. And when he groaned deep in his chest, releasing with primitive abandonment, he held her so tightly, so long, while the tremors waved over him that he did not let go even when he rolled them to their side and his heartbeat slowed.

Later Joan would think of that moment, know, that it did not matter if he didn't turn to her again while they were there. He did not. But neither did he pace and roam the house at night. And he sought her out, and did not shut himself away. He lay beside her, sometimes awake. Most of the time, she knew he was lost in his own thoughts.

When they at last departed, she was thankful for her impulses, and thankful that her heart guided her when experience escaped her in dealing with Roger. She was learning that the man who'd urged her to express herself in London, at the beginning of their affair, the man who could talk so intimately and sexually, sometimes did not want words, or need words, or wish to speak. Sometimes, he would have feelings he could not or was not ready to voice, and would simply need to release those emotions in the most primal and basic way. And Joan, having felt that herself, wholly understood it. The body, she mused, could speak more eloquently than words. He had needed her, and she had been there, and that, for now, was enough.

~

The week prior to the season opening, Roger was away from Lecrox, telling her that his ship had docked, and he'd be aboard should she need anything.

Joan tried not to think possessively, or assume he might be doing otherwise. She made lists, and after finding out that Roger's townhouse was staffed with his father's previous servants, she told Agnes to pack, because she was taking her and her own personal maid along. Then she chose four of his Black Cross servants, sending them ahead with letters for the housekeeper. She might not interfere at his estates, but she bloody well wasn't going to tolerate them at the townhouse, not when she had to play the ton game too.

Roger returned the day before their London trip. She could tell he'd been sailing from the darker shade of his skin, and there were a few scrapes on his hand, a new squint line or two at the corner of his eyes. Still, she'd missed seeing him, and she was glad he had his ship to escape to, glad that he looked much more his familiar self.

"Did Jem take the stud to London?" he asked whilst they were in the bedchamber. He was stripping off his clothing and waiting for the footman to fill the bath.

"Yes. And I sent my gelding." She peeked up from sitting at the secretary, jotting last minute notes. "You look rested for someone who's been out to sea."

He smiled. "I am. O'Brian has become possessive of *The Nighthawk*, he didn't let me do much this go."

"Mmm." She tried to ignore his nudity. "I sent a few servants on with Agnes."

"That's fine." He took a pair of loose cotton trousers from the wardrobe, the type she'd seen sailors wear. "Are you getting your shopping lists done?" He cast her a glance.

"Yes, though I've no real idea of what you normally attend."

"The least I can get by with," he grunted before heading to the bathing room. "I attend my club, the opening ball, and..." he paused and half-turned, "I shall escort you wherever you wish, however, so long as it is *not* a tea or musical."

"Very well." Joan watched the door close and rolled her eyes. *The man acted as if his body had no effect on her when he knew bloody well different.*

It took a few days to get settled in the townhouse, and for Joan to sort through the growing stack of invitations. She knew many were out of curiosity, and some of the hostesses were the worst of the ton gossips, merely old hens who delighted in the next on dit or scandal. She made her list from the most prominent and the high sticklers, whose husbands or sons were either politically influential, or whose invites were more or less a command to appear.

In between, she viewed fashion plates and drew up her orders, going to Bond Street with her maid whilst Wythe was at his club.

One thing she did without consulting her husband, was take stock of the house and begin to change the décor. The colors were cold and the rooms lacking the personal touches that would warm it up. The staff was as she'd expected, but they at least appeared to be meeting her half way after they'd noticed her preference for the Lecrox and Black Cross servants. To her relief, her wishes were followed without any open reserve.

She saw Simon at the end of that first week. He showed up at her breakfast table, having apparently been brought home foxed by Roger the night before.

"Why do you even bother with the season?" She shook her head at him.

"M'father expects at least that much." He sipped the thick coffee and blinked as if trying to unglue his eyes

Joan smiled dryly and looked at Roger. "Can't you save him from his own idiocy?"

"No." Roger was openly amused as the maids brought in steaming platters of food and Simon shuddered and groaned, turning his head away. "He has a head like a bloody rock. He hears what he wishes to."

"Do be fair, Rog. It was not so long ago you were outdoing me."

"I may have, but drinking to the point you do? No."

"I'm merely numbing up for the season."

"Likely you haven't dried out from the last one," Joan muttered and helped herself to eggs. "You're a sporting man, Cousin." She sat back and regarded him. "What sort of wager would it take, to see how long you can stay sober?"

Simon curled his lip. "Do be serious."

"I am. You are a fairly expert sportsman, a good gambler I assume. So I would only pick something that I thought was both challenging, and difficult."

He snorted and glanced at Roger. "Is she serious?"

Roger's glance flickered to his wife. "I think so."

"Well, I hate to disappoint, but I am too well off to wager for money, and not the least inclined to suffer the ton with a clear head."

Joan ate some of her breakfast and wiped her mouth on the pristine napkin, finishing her coffee before saying, "Roger tells me I am more of a challenge at billiards than yourself."

"He bloody well did not." Simon's eyes jerked to Roger.

Wythe shot Joan a chiding look, but said to Simon, "I did, actually."

"And," Joan picked up, "there is a billiard room here, so we shall play after breakfast, since my wardrobe is not ready. If you lose, you must stay sober until the last ball."

Simon snorted. "And if I win?"

She thought a moment. "I'll let you set my debt."

He cocked his brows and glanced at Roger, then back to her. "You are serous."

"Perfectly."

He laughed abruptly and sat back in his chair, eyeing her while he fingered the cup by his plate. "Help me out here, Rog. You likely know her better than I, by now." He looked at his friend and begged, "What should I take advantage of in this situation?"

Roger was looking at Joan, but flickered his gaze to Simon for a split second. "This is between the two of you."

He smiled, and stood, saying before he left, "My money is, of course, on my wife. It would be very un-husbandly of me to bet against her."

"Bloody ass," Simon muttered, but Roger's laughter echoed back as he went through the doors.

Before they left the table, to begin their game, Simon stared at Joan narrow-eyed. "If you were to lose, I should dare you to tell Roger the truth."

"Whatever do you mean?" Her own smile dissipated.

Her cousin's smile was smug. He stood and said succulently, "You are in love with him—and he bloody well does not have a clue."

"Simon—"

"Joan. For all you think my brain is pickled, it is not that fogged. All right, it took me a while after the wedding, to replay everything in my head. But I did put the pieces together and reminded myself of what I knew of you. I also know Rog, have known him for many years, heard his views on marriage, and on love."

Joan sighed. "Trust me. Simon. I know what I am doing. And though I believe you only mean to help him, I will know when it is time to speak my heart."

He shrugged. "Very well. But in case you were wondering, he did not even fall for my attempts to lure him to a certain house of eros…"

"Simon."

He smiled. "It was a small test…"

She stood. "For God sakes, don't tempt him."

He put his arm around her, murmuring, "I'm utterly fascinated by the two of you. Neither of you were exactly eager for wedlock, and I mean this in the best of ways, but you'd have an affair if you wanted him bad enough, as well as tie yourself to a known rake. Rog? Don't even get me started. I'm not reforming, not even close to considering it. But there is something changed in him that is for the better."

"I told you. I am good for him. I do love him, Simon."

"Yes, you did, and you do." He stopped before entering the billiard rooms. "But I think, that Rog is in love with you too.

Joan opened her mouth, half in shock and half in need to ask him how he deduced that? But he stepped away and Roger was in the billiard room. She closed her eyes a moment, taking a steadying breath. *First she had to trounce her cousin well enough to win the bet, then she must give her system time to consider the possibility, that Simon, knowing Rog so well, could possibly be reading what she was missing.*

Chapter 16

Roger positioned himself so that he could observe the competition, seated in a comfortable leather chair, with his feet up, brandy and cigar in hand. From the onset there was a lot of teasing and ribbing, the two cousins loudly trying to distract each other from the shots. He smiled a little watching Simon tie his hair back, declaring he'd missed the first one because it was in his eyes. Joan was making the most of it, crowing over her advantage.

His gaze skimmed down the cream gown she wore, sleeveless and with a snug bodice. He also noted she was in her bare feet. He sighed and leaned his head back against the plush leather, watching from under his lashes as, when she bent or stretched to make her shot, the straight flowing lines of the gown perfectly outlined her pert derrière.

His mind drifted, while his eyes and ears took in their comedy, and he was thinking of the night before, at his club, remembering how many men had come up to him, men who'd known Jordan Lecrox and who had once had a fancy for Anna until the rake had won her hand.

It was just as well Simon had been in his cups and not paying the best attention last night, because Roger had suddenly felt outside the need to get foxed or hear about some new fashionable impure on the scene. He'd had some revelations whilst talking to men who had never approached him before his marriage. One was that very few of them had liked his father, and two was that most had hunted, fished, or traveled with Anna and Jordan. And that man, they had respected greatly, even though Joan's father had lived the bulk of his life away from society's doings.

Another bit of clarity came to his brain when Simon had pushed, prodded, and pressured for him to come with him to a new house of eros. Roger couldn't, at that moment, think of anything or anyone who could rouse him

174

more than Joan. And since they were newly wed, and so much of that time had been darkened by the tour of his estates, there was too much he'd not done with his own wife that he was still looking forward to.

Joan's laughter cut through his thoughts. He focused, seeing that she was half sitting on the table, her bare feet dangling whist she made a shot behind her back. Simon was laughing just as hard and though she missed, her cousin now was determined to outdo her and shot from behind, clipping the eight ball and sending it across the room, almost through the window.

Roger drew on his cheroot, knowing that since that bright day in his father's library, he had pulled back from her. He could read her glances, her silent questions, and he wanted to assure her that he most certainly recalled every second, every feel of her hands and lips and body. He furthermore, still wanted her daily, hourly. But his time on the ship, before preparing to enter the season as a *husband*, had been some much-needed alone time, when he'd asked himself exactly what that word meant, and how seriously he meant to take it.

There were a thousand reasons he didn't want Joan to regret that she'd wed him. And he did not wish to hurt her in any way. Somewhere out at sea, he'd sat on the deck and breathed the salt-tinged air, and realized that that he did not feel shackled or chained or suffocated as he had expected marriage to make him feel.

He felt more free, if anything. Perhaps, free from having to prove something to a dead man, and free from that restlessness that had always nagged at him. His erotic urges too, were centered on Joan, his head filled with vivid images that could have him hard as steel and wanting her at the oddest times. One being…right now.

A year ago he would have reminded her that he was the blackguard that the ton claimed he was. He did not have to do that, because Joan knew nearly everything there was to know, and had wed him anyway.

His eyes landed on her again. Roger thought that *she too was free*, far from being possessed or under his control. Joan's sense of self ruled her daily life, and she did not need a lord and master to instruct her or guide her. Like himself, the only place or time she submitted, was when she chose to and the truest way she expressed her needs and desires, was during those intimate hours when they were alone.

A loud noise jerked him again from his thoughts. Joan was dancing around the billiard table, clapping her hands and shouting loud enough to be heard across the street.

Roger called out, "I take it she won."

Simon, who had broken the cue stick and was half laying across the table, merely cursed and then groaned, vowing revenge.

Before he left the townhouse he told Roger. "I'll honor my losses but do not be surprised if I disappear mid season."

"Where are you going to hide out?" Roger resisted rubbing it in.

"I may as well check on the estates that I so heartily avoid most of the time."

"You're father will be pleased."

"Yes." Simon raked his hair back and yawned. "Just so long as you former rakes don't get it in your head I'm stupid enough to follow suit. I shall be back to my usual sins next season, perhaps I should thank you for leaving the field open?"

"You are welcome to it." Roger snorted. "Just try and keep your head out of a bottle more often when the wager is off."

Simon stared at him. "You know, Rog. I don't have a bloody thing that amuses me anymore. The only damned entertaining thing that happened this year was you and Joan getting hitched."

"Glad I could contribute to interrupting your usual state of boredom." Roger laughed.

"Oh it was, or rather is definitely a highlight."

Roger considered him through the swirl of their cigar smoke. "We've known each other many years Simon. I have no other friends like you. Do take care of yourself."

Simon's brow arched. "Well bloody hell Rog, don't get all sentimental on me." He stood and collected his jacket. "It's mutual," he muttered before going toward the door. "And though I am not speaking to her at the moment, do take care of my cousin...and..."

Roger waited.

Simon sighed and shrugged. "You're a more fortunate chap than you know." He stepped out and shut the door behind him.

~

The opening ball, was a mad crush. Joan fanned herself briskly, trying to waft some fresh air against the lime green ball gown with darker green edging. The taffeta confection was a new design, and Roger had presented her with a set of pearl earrings that went beautifully with it before they'd departed. Her maid had done her curls with tiny pearl pins nestled here and there. She had consciously made an attempt to look like a countess, because she was Roger's wife, and this part of their lives reflected on him, no matter if either of them enjoyed it or not.

Her hand was on his arm, lightly. She had been aware of the turned heads and behind-the-fan whispers when they'd been announced. She took her cue from Roger and ignored it. Since his arrogant way of carrying himself was wholly natural, she pasted a smile on her face, and got through the receiving line without answering a single probing hint from the worst of the lot. Roger, she noticed, didn't bother much with being polite, he bowed, did his greetings and moved on, thankfully taking her with him.

Their first dance together, ever, took place on a crowed ballroom floor. She gazed up at him, mentally registering the fact that for some one who never did so, he was an expert dancer. His strong hand was firm on her spine, and his jet eyes bringing a tad more color to her skin as they tended to center either on her mouth or low bodice.

There was odd dream-like quality to the first hour, not just in the dance, but every time she was introduced as Lady Wythe, or the Countess of Wythe. Joan found the attention a bit too extravagant. But as she'd expected some of it, she fobbed off a few questions between dances with a light laugh and some murmured foolishness about having met him years ago in Bristol.

Her dance card was half full. Roger left her for the card room and some presumably more palatable company than the turbaned dowagers and nosy biddies who were either tapping him with their fan, when she returned to his side, or giving him some scolding look. At one point Joan covered her mouth with her gloved hand, her eyes dancing with amusement when they were trapped in a group of them, all seemingly having no problem approaching or rudely grilling him now that he was wed. Roger had shot her a look between desperation, and annoyance.

Lucky for him, one of the older lords had cut in, dispersing the assemblage, and Roger had escaped to play cards. She however, suffered through it, giving, generally, answers about their estates, and being as polite as possible until her partners showed up. At least when the questions were flying on the dance floor, coming from her male partners whom she assumed neither recalled her from last season, or would dare question Roger, she could pretend breathlessness and avoid a direct answer to their speculations on the rushed marriage and the fact that not one ton member had received an invite.

~

It was well past midnight and the crush only grew while fashionably-late arrivals poured in. After dozens of dances, Joan escaped out the garden doors and politely nodded to other couples and gentlemen who apparently sought the same retreat. She looked up at the stars and then around at the lit gardens, smelling the just-blooming blossoms and sharpness of greenery. She located a bench nestled against a wall, covered in some leafy vine, and sat, pulling off her gloves to give her warm hands some relief, and kicked off her slippers to ease her aching feet.

In the distance Joan could see the main balconies, and below, the sparkle from gowns and jewels as couples strolled the paths. The orchestra music drifted out and the deep yellow luminescence from windows and lampposts scattered along the property.

Three melodies had struck up and faded out while she wondered what Roger was doing. If he was winning, or playing at all. If he was sipping a brandy and chatting with some lord. Or had he caught up with Simon, though she doubted he'd appear until the final hour since he had lost their bet and was in a surly mood.

Joan's gaze drifted and stayed on the curved path to the left, likely an exit from a gentleman's study or the library. She saw the red glow of a cheroot and the dark outline that cast a tall shadow. When he began walking, she recognized her husband's distinct way of carrying himself, and surmised he'd returned to the ballroom to find her, and having not done so he'd guessed right, that she was outside.

He passed under two more lamps. His neck cloth was undone and dangling free, and his hair was unbound and ruffling in the soothing breeze. That familiar tightness, the awareness built as he came closer and each feature was clearer to her eyes. There were times, moments, when she could not fathom the things they had done—she had done—with him, because for all she had wed him, tried to know him, she was a long way from feeling as if he belonged to her. Joan was not as confident as Simon, that Roger was still anything more than in lust, or rather want of her. And time, demands, his distance, had prevented her from having the hours, or lingering in that intimacy where she might have discovered more.

He'd reached the bench. Joan smiled up at him while his black gaze went over her in the moonlight.

His voice was rich, deep when he said, "It's a bloody crush in there."

"Yes. My head was spinning from the lack of breathing room." She shrugged. "And so, the season begins."

He nodded and took a seat beside her, very close and leaning slightly back against the wall.

She glanced aside, finding him studying her. "Did you play cards?"

"A hand or two." He nodded. "Most invitations were nothing more than not so subtle hints to pick my brain."

Joan laughed. "We're the on dit, it seems."

"I've been told a number of times that I'm solely responsible for an astonishing amount in lost wagers." When Joan raised her brow, he supplied. "It seems the bets went on the books last season, when I was suddenly showing up where you were."

"And of course, not one soul would bet, you'd do more than seduce me."

"Mmm. Yes. That's the bulk of the losses. Of course, now they're betting on how long we'll live together, whom I will take for a mistress, and how long before you're carrying the heir, and most presume you already were when we wed."

Joan looked away and toward the mansion. "It's a pity they have nothing better to amuse themselves with."

His hand lifted and she felt it on her back, his fingers trailing down the pattern of embroidery that covered the hooks.

He murmured, "I like this gown."

"Thank you."

"I stood outside the card room a time or two watching you dance, wondering when you'd slip off because your feet hurt."

She laughed, but her eyes were closed, savoring his voice, his touch, his scent and heat beside her. "I suffered through twelve, a new record I think. But one must make allowances for becoming a countess."

His warm fingers went above the material, lightly touching the tops of her shoulder blades where the wide neckline exposed them. "Marriage has turned out to have an inordinate amount of demands that have provided us the opposite of what we set out to gain."

His finger and thumb undid one hook, and then two, and at the third and the loosening of her bodice, Joan whispered, "There are couples walking this way."

But his hand slid inside and around, nudging her until he was cupping her breast and massaging it. He leaned his head down and dragged his warm mouth down the side of her neck.

Loins immediately reacting, Joan moaned softly and instinctively positioned to give him the most freedom, even while her heart was thumping deeply and fast, her skin tingling. She turned her head into his next kiss, and opened for his tongue to slide inside. The sensual contractions rippled through her inner muscles with each stroke, each taste, and painfully so when he squeezed lightly at her nipple.

Exhaling trembling air from nostrils, she kissed him back aggressively seeking more flavor and a deeper taste.

His mouth lifted an inch before turning to graze her ear, which he bit before rasping, "You feel like warm silk, love. And taste of womanly hungers."

"I am hungry." She caught her breath when he cupped the globe firmly. "Roger, my... God," she was starting to tremble.

He pulled her back against him, slid the shoulder strap down until the milky skin and rose tip glowed in the moonlight. Tracing it, rolling the nipple in his fingers, he breathed against her throat, and laved a spot just under her ear before nuzzling that breast.

"I...hear someone...coming," Joan panted unable to look away from those dark lips on her breast.

He stole a quick taste, enough to leave the tip quivering and wet, and then returned her so that it appeared they were merely sitting side by side.

Only Joan was fully aware that his hand was still on her skin.

A couple she vaguely recalled from her first season glanced over on their stroll up the path, nodding and speaking, but only Roger spoke because Joan was too focused on keeping her arms down to stop her bodice from falling.

When they were several feet away, she sighed and glanced at her husband. "Are you mad? We may be wed but that was—it was risky."

His white teeth gleamed in the shadows. "You enjoyed every moment of it."

"Of course I did." Her eyes widened and she hissed laughing, "You know what happens when you touch me."

He moved his hand and redid the hooks, murmuring, "It has been awhile, I thought to refresh our memory."

"There's not a bloody thing wrong with mine." Joan stood while she had the chance, trying to steady her knees. She faced him wearing a scolding smile. "Roger, I've got another hour to get through and you've...well, you know what you've done."

He chuckled, and leaned up, his hands skimming the material from her knees to her thighs. "There's nothing wrong with anticipation."

She leaned her head back drawing in a deep breath. Finally she moaned softly, "I've wanted you for weeks, days. I ache."

He was on his feet in seconds, taking her in his arms and kissing her hungrily. This time when he lifted his head, she was completely limp against him.

"Well that bloody well helped."

His mouth touched her ear, "You have an hour to think of where you want my mouth and these hands." He caressed her buttocks. "Tonight is yours, love, until every hunger is satisfied, and every ache soothed."

"Roger." She moaned against his shirtfront. "I can't even walk."

He laughed and slid his arm around her. Joan leaned into his side, her palm on his stomach as they walked out of the shadows. Before entering the ballroom, she drew a steady breath and pulled away from him. Glancing up as she slipped her arm through his. "Your neck cloth is untied."

He shrugged and winked. "We may as well give them fuel for the fire."

Everything seemed loud and glaring to Joan once they were amid the crowd again. The orchestra was, the voices trying to talk over it were, and the lights sparkling, dancing off jeweled gowns and encrusted hair-bands, seemed too much for her eyes.

As decorum dictated she kept a distance between herself and her husband, and Roger did relent enough to retie his neck cloth, if simply, and lead her in another dance.

It was too long an hour. Joan wanted to run to the coach by the time they were ready to depart. He may not have touched her, but Roger's eyes were on her throughout that hour.

Inside the coach, she tucked her gloves into the pocket of her cape and laid it aside. Her husband sat across from her, elbow on the window and dark eyes glowing in her direction. Sexual tension thickened the air. It coiled inside her. She lifted the window flap and looked out, wondering that her body came alive so quickly, that her blood hummed in her veins and her heart was racing with anticipation. Roger knew that, the wretch, he had to know that by now.

When they arrived at the townhouse, Joan smiled stiffly at the footmen, the butler, and her maid, who helped her undress upstairs. The pins were removed from her hair. It was combed to a natural spring of curls around her head. Absent the ball gown, she sponged off in cool, scented water, pleased that she'd changed the colors in the master suite to jade and ivory silk, and absently listening to Roger and his valet in the adjoining room, attending to his toilette.

Betsy had lit the lamps and turned them up so that the richness of the fabrics shimmered and the polished floors gleamed under the tawny glow. Sliding on a silk robe of black and crimson, Joan mentally moaned at the caress of it on her sensitive skin, and walked over to the padded window seat to pull back the drapes and open it to the early morning air.

She was standing there, one knee on the cushion, and allowing the fog misted breeze to waft over her, when Roger entered.

He padded over, barefoot and wearing the loose linen trousers he preferred to lounge in. He came close behind her, touching and warm, solid and smelling of that night wind and mysterious maleness that stirred her senses. He rested his chin atop her head, sliding his arms around her in an embrace.

"I await your desire."

She sighed, shaky. "Do I have to verbalize it?"

"No. But it will please me to hear it." He slid his head down and kissed her neck. "And it will make you more aroused to say it."

"I am near begging now."

He bit her neck. "Begging for what, love?"

"For anything you want to give me."

He kissed the spot, then raised and turned her to face him. "You want to be taken?"

"Taken?" She was hot inside and out. *Yes. Take me,* she thought.

184

"You want me to take you?" He fisted the front of her robe and stared at her. "You want to be ravished. To be devoured, and to burn, hotter, higher..."

Joan felt her blood flame. It totally surprised her that she indeed did want more of that aggression she saw in his eyes. For a panicked moment she wondered just how much a man like him knew of such things, and how far he'd go.

He whispered, "You may trust me, love. I will not harm you. I will give you more than you can stand and twice what you desire. Now, tell me."

She wet her lips. Her eyes pinned to his. "I'm...not afraid. I'm just not sure how to put it."

He reached down with his other hand and slid her robe belt off. Taking it he led her to the bed and, bound her hands to a comfortable snugness, just enough to be sexually dominating without actually hurting her.

"This?"

She swallowed. "Yes."

His face because intense. His voice deepened. He glanced down at the gaping robe before he whispered, "And?"

"As I did to you, on our wedding night."

His eyes burned into hers. "Do you trust me?"

"Yes."

Roger left her and turned down three of the lamps, leaving the bed in a pool of light before he came, and leaned her over. He was staring down at her when he grasped the material and ripped the flimsy robe completely off her back.

Joan trembled, her breath hissed through her clenched teeth.

He lifted her, poised her on her knees at the headboard. He spread her arms wide...and secured them to the posts, his eyes constantly going to her face, as her breathing grew loud and her body trembled harder.

With her back and buttocks against the smooth wood, her knees wide and sitting on her heels, Joan watched him strip and slide upon the bed until he faced her. He leaned down delicately touching his tongue to her aching nipples so painfully light she was, before long, arching forward and trying to force more of his tongue onto them.

But he would not give more except to apply the tip of his tongue down between them, down to the top of her curls before sitting up again. Chills spread over her skin, and she hissed louder when he softly touched her curls, barely stroking, through them.

"Please..." she moved her hips trying to get more of the touch.

"What do you want?'

"I want you to touch me harder."

He gave her what she wanted, but swiftly and fully and with friction so intense she leaned her head back gulping air.

He stopped and his touch left her.

"Roger!"

He leaned up, found her mouth and began an explicit kiss that turned into him sucking her tongue deep into his mouth. He slid his lips down it, and he reached between her legs and touched her moist heat, sliding his finger into her, while he ravaged her mouth.

Joan was moaning, not caring how loud. He lifted his head. But he moved to her breasts, this time sucking hard, at both, before sliding down in the bed. He bit and laved from her inner knee to her groin, each time coming close, but not giving the touch she wanted. He slid his hands back, under her, with his thumbs between her buttocks and rubbing every sensitive nerve, until she was muttering and trying to move against him.

He kissed everywhere then, laving and sucking and biting softly until she heard herself pleading. Joan sobbed with relief when he finally centered his attentions between her curls, aggressively, with moans and rumbles in his throat, he drank and suckled and ate her, to the point the climax came without warning, exploding on a half drawn breath that made her feel like her heart had burst.

Before her head cleared, he was inside her. On his knees, his hands gripping the headboard and shaft driving deep, fast, hard. She came again, in a drawn-out compression of intense pleasure, her cry of his name turning into a whisper. He took her over the edge once more, before she could drift down to earth.

Joan blinked, aware that he was still. That their bodies were locked tightly together. She looked up at him.

Roger began to move again, in hard, and out slow, his body all but lifting hers off the bed.

"My...God," she choked, feeling the orgasm building. "I..."

"Yes, yes...' He slid his hands down, grasping her hips. "Feel me. All the way, Joan. Come on, love, reach for it. Take it."

"I do. I am. This is...Oh...don't stop."

He slammed hard and reached out to untie the bonds. But when she would have embraced him he turned her around, retied them, and entered her from behind. There was nothing but his body driving flashes of pleasure through her. He was hard, demanding, and roughly sensual, and Joan was lost. A blur of white heat engulfed her. Each thrust and each stroke of his sex was better than the one before. Her awareness became one continual elevation of intensity and his driving thrusts so uninterrupted, a ceaseless barrage of his sex stroking hers, she was too far gone to know, when he shuddered and came. And she was still fogged when he'd untied her and washed his seed from her thighs.

Half of the hour she lay there, spent, simply assimilating what it had felt like to be taken by him. By the time the flashbacks had stirred her blood, he was leading her to the window seat and taking her again, holding her arms up against the wall and leaving her no choice but to trust he could hold them both up while he took her body to the absolute edge, and finally over, the crest of fulfillment.

Chapter 17

Dawn's chill pervaded the room. They lay again on the bed, silent. Joan rolled her head to gaze at him. Thinking her eyes would never tire of doing so. He was on his side, facing her.

She felt peculiar, not exactly embarrassed, but rather taken aback that she'd enjoyed that so much. She was also wondering what he thought of her now. And wondering if he felt any differently about her. Pondering if it was something in her that trusted him that much, or something in her that needed to be...receptive. *Yes, there was a part of her that wanted that,* while still feeling brazen, bold. But it was about him too, and how she felt about him, how she needed to feel him that intensely, that strongly, that powerfully inside of her...

Roger was watching her face, reading her eyes, when he reached out and languidly stroked her cheek. "You are ready for something sweeter now, shall I take you to a place of sunrises?" he whispered softly, "be the fragrance of morning wind, the repose of opalescent clouds, all the warm colors of your heaven?" He leaned down, kissed her light and tender, stroking her body with soothing touches and loving caresses, gliding his hands up her arms, over her back, her throat, and down her stomach.

There was a hushed ebb and flow, a reverent kind of adoration to each touch and sensation. He brushed his cheek across her belly, her breasts, lightly tasting her skin, blowing feathery kisses upon it.

Moments later he eased into her slowly, carefully, exquisitely planting kisses on her brow, her cheek, and under her ear. As he glided inside and back, his hand sometimes drifted, down her leg, up her thigh, smooth and stroking, drawn out and airy-light, caressing.

Joan felt tears scald her eyes. They rolled down, into her hair. She held him and stroked his back and sides, sensed and felt the gentle tenderness of his every moment, the deliberate intent and emotion in every flex of his body.

The tears gathered, thickened, until her throat was locking with the build-up of her emotions. Where he had eased her fire before, he was touching her body, heart and soul now. Her heart—it was expanding in her chest, swelling fuller until she held him still shuddering, her mouth at his throat when she cried softly, "I'm sorry. So sorry." She sobbed and held him tight.

"Joan?" His body froze in motion.

"I'm sorry." She was openly crying now, and resisted when he tried to unlock her hands from him, not wanting him to move from her, not wanting him to see her face.

But her sobs and the deep sound of her crying was not to be ignored. Roger succeeded in moving her arms from around him, and slid down so that he could look at her, holding her face still with his palms when she tried to turn it away.

"Joan what is wrong? My God, did I hurt you before?"

"No. No. It was wonderful. Everything is with you." She reached up and tried to wipe her eyes. Looking at him through a blur.

"Why are you crying? Why are you apologizing?"

Her body shuddered against his and she sniffed in air, trying to get hold of herself, but recognizing that falling apart sensation, knowing that she was going to, whether she wanted to or not. "Nothing, everything." She pulled at his wrists. "Please…just…I'm sorry."

When he let go, she moved from him and lay on her stomach, her forehead against her forearm.

His hand was splayed on her spine. He was leaning over her when he husked, "I promised not to hurt you."

"You didn't hurt me."

His tone was tense. "Then what the hell is wrong? You don't cry for nothing."

"It's just a woman's thing. Just stupid emotions."

He lay down close, his hand still on her back. "Look at me."

"Not yet. Not now." She turned her head opposite and reached up to wipe her eyes. She even forced a laugh. "I'm sorry. I didn't mean to start blubbering like an idiot."

"That doesn't matter, love. What does, is why. Now, turn around and talk to me."

Joan bit down on her lip and closed her eyes. She breathed in deep several times, wiping her eyes and sniffing back emotions before she felt she could obey. She rolled to her back, meeting his ready gaze when she did so. In a thick voice she whispered, "This isn't going to happen every time."

"I certainly hope not." He traced her brow. "It gives a man pause when he is deep inside his woman's body, and she is weeping rather than moaning his name in ecstasy."

Her chuckle was watery. "Another new experience for you?"

"I'll say." He smiled tensely and rested his fingertips on her jaw, turning her more fully to face him. "Getting words out of you is like pulling teeth, love. You are more guarded than I, with your feelings."

"I'm sorry."

"Which means nothing." He shook his head. "Christ, Joan. I am not the easiest man in the world to tolerate, I know my flaws, and so I think, do you. But you would not let me sink into them and brood. You turned an otherwise gloomy tour of the estates into a rather erotic memory for me."

"Did I?"

"Yes." He smiled. "I have awoken a dozen times re-dreaming it and hard enough to avoid the valet a good hour in the morning."

Joan smiled. "I'm glad. I rather enjoyed it too."

"We are married, lovers, I have wicked plans for your body. We have a massive bed at Black Cross with all sorts of delightful secrets to explore. We haven't had that much time. Not enough to begin to ease our desire for each other, and to dull the edge of this intense spark that flares whenever we are within touching distance." He paused a breath, then confessed, "But I bloody well can't think of that when I was attempting to give you sweetness and made you cry."

She closed her eyes, and took his hand from her face, kissing his palm before she sat and slid up against the headboard.

Dawn was in fullness. The smell of coal fires drifted in on the fog. Joan wrapped her arms around her knees, and kept her gaze on those wisps drifting through the window.

"I'm in love with you." She cleared her throat and looked down, before glancing at him where he still lay with his head on the pillow, one arm supporting it. "I'm sorry. I know that everything was supposed to be about freedom, about remaining ourselves and having no expectations beyond the sexual." She wet her lips and looked away again. "I was in love with you before I left London. I knew when you asked me to wed, that I shouldn't. I felt, well, I knew that it was a foolish risk to take. That I was eventually going to feel it. In one of those moments when you touched me, and all of my defenses were down."

An unsteady sigh escaped Joan as she rested her forehead on her knees. "I loved you enough to *not* want to marry you, just because I may have been with child. I loved you enough to think that I could feel it and agree to wed you for the reasons we did anyway." She whispered, "The thing is, Roger. I'm not a little girl any more." Her eyes burned and filled again. "There's no father to tell me wonderful lies and make it go away. There's no telling myself it's a dream, and not real and it should not happen. Because it did happen, and I can't make it go away." She lifted her head and wiped her eyes. "My eyes were open. But so was my heart."

192

She rested her elbows on her knees and pressed her aching eyes into the heels of her hands. "I don't want you leave me. I don't care why or how, or anything. I don't want you to leave me, please, Roger." She began to weep again. "I will never ask anything else of you, I promise. Just be where I am and let me love you."

"Joan." The sound was torn from his chest as he raised and gathered her close, holding her tight against his trembling body.

"Don't say anything, please don't say anything." She held on and cried so hard for so long, that he was sure the servants heard.

In fact the valet opened the adjoining door with Roger's coffee, and Wythe snarled, "Get out!"

The cups shook on the tray. The servant set it on a table and hurried out the door.

He could not get another sound out of his throat. He held onto Joan, her words ripped through his body, his heart and soul like an explosion, tearing down walls and splintering armor, shaking him to the core.

Roger closed his eyes, feeling every sob and every breath that came from her. Feeling the truth, until vividly the lucidity that came when the chaos inside him dissipated, was like a fresh breath of air that cleansed his lungs, and awakened him out of a sleep.

~

Joan slept late and awoke in the late afternoon, to have her bath and prepare for another season's appointment. She did not see Wythe, and was informed that he was at his club, and would return to escort her.

She refused to think about why her head was heavy, and why she did not feel like doing anything but returning to Lecrox, where she could walk and think and be, without having to paste on smiles and pretend life was one long ball.

She bathed and let Betsy dress her in gold silk and do her hair with topaz pins. Her gold velvet cloak and white gloves, her fan, were all laid out when she heard Roger return, and heard him dressing in the next chamber.

She sipped her third coffee, standing by the window, hoping that Roger would let her confession pass without comment. Hoping he'd put it down to some woman's silliness, even if she deplored being thought of as weak.

The click of the door drew her head around, and she barely skimmed Roger visually before setting down her cup. She didn't need to stare to know he looked handsome in the formal clothing, and that when they left the ball for the opera, he was going to draw plenty of female eyes. And her stomach was going to be in knots.

He had walked to the bed and held her cloak for her. She slipped it on, pulling on her gloves as they left the room. Joan ticked off the movements in her head as she walked down the stairs, smiling at a worried-looking Agnes, nodding to the butler, then the footman, and finally sitting in the coach.

Traffic was thick, a good distraction, so Joan kept her gaze out the window. Tension had crawled over her skin by the time they were at the ball. Joan danced with Roger, she danced with men she did not even see, and when it was time to depart for the play, she was brittle enough to have trouble breathing.

The Earl of Wythe's box afforded a perfect view of the stage. Joan declined champagne before the show, and took her seat, again, knowing without looking that Wythe had left to have a cheroot and brandy before the play began.

The target of eyes and turned opera glasses, she sat with false ease, her gloved hands in her lap, one holding her fan, and her gaze only flickering occasionally toward a noisy group.

She did flinch when the orchestra struck up, and released a tense breath as the lights went down. Looking under her lashes at him when Roger entered and took his seat beside her, she mentally urged the curtains to open, for the play to start.

It was a moving drama, a piece where the music soared to loud heights and plunged to deep and dark depths. It relayed the potent mood of the scenes, and seemed to sweep the audience into the center of the storm rather swiftly. Joan was aware the moment that Roger was no longer watching the stage. She felt the intensity of his gaze for the full first act.

By the third, she was praying for it to end, to be at home and to be somewhere that she could find her old humor and lightness of spirit. To be somewhere she could let go of that deeply held breath, relax her tense stomach and find her balance once more.

The very last scene, the very last act, her fingers bit into the fan. She thought herself completely mad when she heard the first whisper.

"I love you, Joan."

Her heart stopped in her chest. Her breath poised in her lungs. Joan tried to hear the actor's words, thinking that she had inserted her own name and Roger's voice in them.

But again that distinct sound caressed her ear, and it was Roger's voice when he repeated, "I love you."

Her eyes rolled slightly. Their lids lowered.

Amid the thunder of applause, the whistles and shouts of the audience, the calls and cacophony—

"I love you...I love you...I love you."

The tears that scalded now were silent, thin streams that forced her to open her eyes. The lights came up and she arose on shaky legs, feeling him help her with her cape, take her by the arm, and lead her to the coach.

"I love you, Joan."

She felt the sway of the coach, heard the crush of wheels and through tears, saw the distorted amber of passing street lamps.

They arrived home. He helped her down. She nodded to the butler, moved up the stairs and sent the maid from her room. Dropping her cloak and gloves on the floor,

Joan stumbled to the window seat and pushed the shutters wide. Burying her face against her arms on the ledge, she drew in shuddered breaths, one after the other trying to catch her breath.

Roger entered through the connecting door.

She squeezed her eyes tightly closed and felt each step that brought him closer to her.

He sat beside her, and put his hand on her trembling back. "I love you."

She laughed on a sob, raised her head, turning to him, and throwing herself into his arms, holding him tightly and whispering back, "I love you. With everything I have, Roger. I love you."

His hand splayed on the back of her head, and he used it to ease her back for his kiss. A lush kiss, that was full and silken, that went on and on, while he unhooked her gown and managed to get her completely nude in his arms.

Joan filled her lungs when he laid her on the bed, then he stole her breath again as he stripped and joined her, gathering her under him, and making love to her as he had begun the night before. This time, with whispers in her ear that came from his heart and his very soul, he gave her what he'd refused all others, and took into himself what no one but Joan knew how to give.

In a moment of extreme pleasure, a second, poised on the brink of release, Joan caught his gaze. Their eyes locked. Heartbeat against heartbeat, she felt the depth, the truth flood through her. His eyes burned, face quiescent and his seed spilled deep in her womb. She saw him luxuriate in the surrender and submerge in the ecstasy.

Epilogue - Three years later

"Roger, are you sure this is safe?" Joan eyed the rope ladder before she spied the crow's nest of *The Nighthawk*.

A toddler son on one hip, cradling a year old daughter on the other, he assured with a laugh. "Yes. Cully is up there too, don't worry."

She grimaced. "When did I say I wanted to do this again?"

Her son piped up. "When Da' yelled at you to please stop screaming, when Anna was being borned, because he was bloody well going to kill Agnes for barring the damn door, and it took three footmen—"

"That's enough, Son," Roger cut him off dryly. He looked at his wife, lingering a bit on her trousers and billowing white shirt. "You know bloody well you lost a wager to me before we even made Anna."

Her lip curled. "Yes, right-oh—I did, didn't I?"

"But if you are actually frightened, love…"

"No, no. I am perfectly fine." She drew a bracing breath. "If I don't do it whist I have this chance I shall be too old, or pregnant again, to have a go at it."

Roger muttered, "We're taking a break from that for a while."

Foot on the rung she whirled and blinked. "I beg your bloody pardon?"

"Not *that*." He laughed loudly and winked. "You get no mercy on that score. I meant these little creatures we made who, if not for four nurses and a whole floor of Black Cross, would see that we don't have a moment's privacy."

"Wot?" His son's black brow rose. "I beg your bloody pardon?"

Both Joan and Roger fell into peals of laughter, Joan hanging onto the rope and shaking her head at the lad's wit.

When he'd gathered himself Roger muttered, "You are not going to accomplish this today, love. Come, let's give your son something better to do than mimic every word we say."

But Joan had started up the rope, and halfway she called down to Roger, "I just had a wickedly delicious idea."

He eyed the crow's nest and judged the size and stability. "You make it up there, darling, and I'll promise you a view you'll never forget."

Her laughter floated down as she scurried up, and took the sailors hand and then was at last in the crow's nest.

For a long moment Joan simply remained awed by the height, the feel of the wind and wonderful freedom. She asked the seaman, "Can I see those spy glasses?"

"'elp yerself." He grinned and took them off the hook and handed them to her.

She scanned the ocean with the magnified view, followed the soar of a sea gull and caught her breath at the beauty of a sunset.

A sharp, piercing whistle caused her to jump.

The sailor tapped her on the shoulder. "Down below milady."

She arced the spyglasses to the deck, and screamed.

Roger, having given the children over to the crew to watch, was taking his bloody clothing off...

"He wouldn't..." she choked, seeing his shirt flutter off and then his boots were gone. "He won't..." she screamed when his hands went to his trousers.

"This be where I take my leave." The sailor laughed and hopped lithely, to catch the sail and slide downward—because Roger was climbing up to the crow's nest, completely naked.

When he reached the platform, wearing little but a wicked smile, Joan finally snapped her gaping mouth shut.

"Hello, my love."

Joan's smiled bloomed. Her eyes danced. "Roger, you're completely daft."

He stepped close to her. "Is the view...stirring?"

Her eyes went down him. "I'm completely breathless...with awe."

His hand reached for her trouser flap and murmured, "I'll do the talking for the both of us then." His fingers touched her.

Joan closed her eyes. "Yes." She felt him slide the trousers off and lift her up.

"Just a whisper, darling, just a word from your heart."

He held her tightly joined to him, his mouth against her ear, whispering "I love you, Joan...I love you...I love you..."

She did soar then, higher, freer, lighter than the wind, and safely held, guided by that one voice, one sound, that knew how to make her feel alive and wonderfully adored. The mate of her heart, soul, and body. And when her eyes opened, there was the face of the man who made the darkness heavenly, and the shadows before dawn, the most magnificent to behold...

The End

About the Author:

Gayle Eden and Eve Asbury are the pen names for Dian Addair, an author whose dreams of writing were put on hold in her twenties while she raised a son and daughter and worked several jobs. Romance novels kept her sane during those busy years during which she moved from the mountains of West Virginia to a suburb of Washington DC where she lived for fifteen years. Finally, she settled in East Tennessee (USA) on three acres surrounded by the North Holston River, where she now writes to her heart's content.

Already a grandmother at 44, she calls her life controlled chaos, but it's actually quite normal for a woman who was born 9th in line and was an aunt by the age of five. She sets aside Saturdays for family, cooking and romping with the granddaughters. The rest of the week, when not stealing an hour with her busy husband, she spends at the computer immersing herself in another good plot.

She's an author who believes very strongly in writing stories that speak from the heart. She tries not to limit her characters by outline, but starts with a vague idea that generally they will run away with - and sometimes give her fits by defying her attempts to keep them in check. It's not unheard of for her to sit down at the computer and realize ten hours later she's written 200 pages—prolific, yes! She's found it's better to indulge her muse than try to control it. Just like real life, the stories happen, and there's always something new and surprising that makes the experience rewarding.

gayle.eden@lindenbayromance.com

Other works by Gayle Eden:

Rock My World

Raelyn Kendell, a washed-up singer, is summoned home when her brother is injured in a bull riding accident. Raelyn is tough as nails on the outside and has had to face more than her share of sorrow and failure. She knows she'll have to face her father, who's predictions of her failure have come true. What she doesn't know is that she's going to come face-to-face with Hud McKabe.

The attraction between Raelyn and Hud is immediate and fiery. They want one another. They can't stand one another. Sparks turn to passion and then somewhere along the way, as Raelyn works through the splintered relationships of her past and Hud breathes life back into her dreams, passion becomes love.

This fabulous story by Gayle Eden is about finding your way home, finding yourself, and finding that guy--the one you were meant to be with forever. All he has to do is look and you know…He's gonna Rock My World.

The Fox

The Industrial Revolution is underway and England has never been so modern or progressive. Blaire Mitchell, a good woman in a desperate situation, is faced with an age-old dilemma. With no skills, no money, and no power she's the only one left who can save her family farm and her brother. In order to succeed she must clear the enormous debts left behind by her parents. Determined to do whatever it takes and to make any sacrifice, Blaire strikes a deal that will change her life forever.

Gabriel Wynters is the notorious Fox, a gambling hall owner who is as ruthless as he is clever. Gabriel strikes a deal with the lovely and innocent Blaire, her virtue and one night in his bed in exchange for the money she so badly needs. But Blaire offers more than her body. With her, he experiences a closeness and intimacy unlike ever before. Although he thought one taste would be enough for him, Blaire gets under his skin and manages to tug on his heart.

The Fox is a story about a love that is boundless, a love that is consuming. Gabriel and Blaire start out as partners and lovers in a unique arrangement. But they soon grow to realize that what they truly desire is to belong to one another utterly, completely, and in every way.

This is a publication of
Linden Bay Romance
WWW.LINDENBAYROMANCE.COM

Recommended Linden Bay Romance Read:

Trust and Treason by Donna MacQuigg

Young and naïve, Elizabeth Rothwell always dreamed that she would marry for love and live the rest of her life in Thornhill Castle. When Elizabeth is given in marriage to the fearsome Scottish Chieftain, Robert MacDairmid, those hopes are dashed.

Robert is a man filled with the need for vengeance. To obtain the means to destroy the man responsible for the death of his wife and child, he agrees to marry Elizabeth, his enemy's beautiful niece.

Although Elizabeth fears she will never be able to compete with the memories of Robert's past, she is determined to try, and surrenders herself completely. The powerful warrior, with his gentle caresses and breath-stealing kisses, awakens in her an explosive passion, and earns her heart.

Elizabeth is put to the test when Robert's plot to free Scotland from English rule unfolds. When Robert is sentenced to death for treason, Elizabeth is faced with a choice. Does she dismiss everything that's happened between them and believe that she was nothing more to Robert than a political pawn? Or, should she trust once more in her feelings, forgive Robert's act of treason, and fight to save the man she loves?